COUPERUS

FATE

Fredonia Books
Amsterdam, The Netherlands

Fate

by
Louis Marie Anne Couperus

ISBN: 1-4101-0393-5

Copyright © 2003 by Fredonia Books

Fredonia Books
Amsterdam, The Netherlands
http://www.fredoniabooks.com

In order to make original editions of historical works
available to scholars at an economical price, this
facsimile of the original edition is reproduced from
the best available copy and has been digitally
enhanced to improve legibility, but the text remains
unaltered to retain historical authenticity.

CONTENTS

FATE

Contents

LIFE OF COUPERUS

FROM Louis Marie Anne Couperus, now aged but forty-three, his masterpiece is yet to be expected. This is the opinion of several critics, among them Edmund Gosse, who, like his colleagues, thinks very highly of "Fate." The publication of this, his first novel, drew down upon Couperus the displeasure of Holland's religious papers; one of them alleged that the book in question was responsible for a young man's suicide, while others clamored for the institution of a national Index Expurgatorius, so that all such pernicious literature might be safely disposed of. "Eline Vere," a much longer story, was published a year later, namely, in 1892, and "Ecstasy" was brought out about the same time. In 1894 appeared "Majesty," which through its serial publication in the principal Dutch review, "De Nieuwe Gids," substantially improved the fortunes of that magazine. Curiously enough, the well-known French author Jules Lemaître coincidently wrote a novel on a

3

similar theme, naming it "Kings." "Majesty" was followed by a double sequel, "Universal Peace" and "Primo Cartello," and in 1901 "Little Aims" was put into print.

Couperus's first literary endeavors did not, however, take the form of prose. His virgin volume, so to speak, was a collection of poems entitled "Orchids," presented to the Dutch public when the author was twenty-four years old. The fervent tone and glowing Oriental imagery of these verses one may partly attribute to the young man's early residence in the East Indies, at Batavia, where his father occupied an official post under the Dutch Government. It is said that the author of "Fate," who was born at The Hague on the 10th of June, 1863, is of Scottish ancestry, his surname being really a Latinized form of "Cowper."

FATE

CHAPTER I

HIS hands in his pockets, and the collar of his fur coat turned up, Frank was making his way one evening, through squalls of snow, along the deserted length of Adelaide Road. As he approached the villa where he lived—White-Rose Cottage, it was called—sunk, buried, wrapped in white snow, like a nest in cotton wool, he was aware of some one coming to meet him from Primrose Hill. He looked steadily in the man's face, since he evidently intended to address him, doubting as to what his purpose might be this lonely, snowy night, and he was greatly surprised when he heard said in Dutch:

"Pardon the intrusion. Are you not Mr. Westhove?"

"Yes," replied Frank Westhove. "Who are you? What do you want?"

"I am Robert van Maeren. You may perhaps remember—"

"What! you, Bertie?" cried Frank. "How came you here in London?"

5

Fate

And in his amazement there rose up before him, through the driving snow, a vision of his youth; a pleasing picture of boyish friendship, of something young and warm.

"Not altogether by chance," said the other, whose voice had taken a somewhat more confident tone at the sound of the familiar "Bertie." "I knew that you lived here, and I have been to your door three times; but you had not come in. Your maid said that you were expected at home this evening, so I made so bold as to wait here for you." And again his voice lost its firmness and assumed the imploring accent of a beggar.

"Is your business so urgent, then?" asked Frank in surprise.

"Yes. I want—perhaps you could help me. I know no one here—"

"Where are you living?"

"Nowhere. I only arrived here early this morning, and I have—I have no money."

He was shivering from standing in the cold during this short dialogue, and seemed to shrink into himself, almost fawning, like a cowed dog.

"Come in with me," said Frank, greatly astonished, but full of sympathy and of the affectionate reminiscences of his boyhood. "Come and spend the night with me."

"Oh, gladly!" was the reply, eager and tremulous, as if he feared that the heaven-inspired words might be retracted.

They went together a few steps further; then Frank took a key out of his pocket, the key of White-Rose Cottage. He opened the door; a hexagonal Moorish lantern was burning low, and shed a soft light in the hall.

"Go in," said Frank. And he locked the door and bolted it behind them. It was half-past twelve.

The maid had not yet gone to bed.

"That gentleman called here a little while ago, two or three times," she murmured, with a look of suspicion at Bertie. "And I have seen him hanging about all the evening, as if he was on the watch. I was frightened, do you know; it is so lonely in these parts."

Frank shook his head reassuringly.

"Make the fire up as quickly as possible, Annie. Is your husband still up?"

"The fire, sir?"

"Yes. Bertie, will you have something to eat?"

"Gladly, if it gives you no trouble," replied Bertie in English, for the benefit of the maid, and he looked with an insinuating expression to meet the surprised, cold blue eyes of the neat, brisk young woman. His voice was persuasive and low; he tried to take as little room as possible in the small hall; and to avoid her gaze, he seemed to

Fate

shrink, to efface himself in a corner where the shadow fell.

Frank led the way into a large back room, cold and dark when they entered, but soon lighted up, and before long genially warmed by the huge fire which blazed up in the grate. Annie laid the table.

"Supper for one, sir?"

"Lay for two; I will eat something," said Frank, thinking that Bertie would feel more at his ease.

At his friend's invitation the visitor had seated himself in a large armchair by the fire, and there he sat, bolt upright, without speaking, feeling shy before the woman, who came and went. And now, in the light, Frank could see the poverty of his appearance; his thin, shabby coat, shining with grease and bereft of buttons; his worn, fringed trousers; his dirty comforter, hiding a lack of underlinen; his ripped and slipshod shoes. In his confusion and awkwardness he still held his battered hat. This garb accorded ill with the aristocratic elegance of his figure; the thin, pale, chiseled features, full of distinction in spite of the unkempt light hair and unshaven stubble of beard. It was like a masquerade of rank and culture in the rags of misery, beseeming it as ill as an unsuitable part in a play. And the actor sat motionless, staring into the fire, ill at ease in the atmosphere of luxury which surrounded him in this room, evi-

Fate

dently the home of a young man of fortune, who had no yearnings for domestic society. The curtains and carpets were of handsome quality, so were the furniture and ornaments, but arranged without any reference to comfort; the chairs and tables against the wall, stiff and orderly, and shining with polish. But it did not make this impression on Bertie, for a sense of the blessedness of warmth and shelter possessed him wholly; of peace and reprieve, as calm as a lake and as delightful as an oasis—a smiling prospect after the snow and cold of the last few hours. And when he saw that Frank was gazing at him in visible wonder at his motionless attitude by the glorious fire, where the dancing flames flew up like yellow dragons' tongues, at last he smiled, and said with humble gratitude in the tone of a beggar:

"Thank you very much—this is good—"

Annie had not much to set before them: the remains from the larder of a young fellow who lives chiefly away from home—a bit of cold beefsteak and salad, some biscuits and jam; but it bore some resemblance to a supper, and Bertie did it full honor, eating and drinking with systematic deliberateness, hardly conscious of what; and imbibing hot grog without confessing the hunger which had nipped his very vitals. At length Frank tried to make him speak, drew him into talk, and into telling him what had reduced him to such misery. Bertie told his tale in a fragmentary fashion, very abjectly, every word sounding like a petition:

Disputes with his father about his mother's fortune—a trifle of a few thousand gulden quickly spent; vicissitudes in America, where he had been by turns a farm-servant, a waiter in a hotel, and a *super* on the stage; his return to Europe on board a liner, working out his passage in every variety of service; his first day in London—without a cent. He remembered Westhove's address from letters bearing date of some years back, and had at once made his way to White-Rose Cottage, only fearing that meanwhile Frank might have moved half a dozen times, and left no traces—

Oh! his anxiety that night, waiting in the cold wind, while it grew darker and darker; the gloom, with no relief but the ghostly whiteness of the deathly silent snow! And now, the warmth, the shelter, and food! And again he thanked his friend, cowering, shriveled, in his threadbare clothes.

"Thank you, thank you—"

Annie, sulky over so much trouble at this hour of the night, and for such a vagabond brought in from the street, had nevertheless prepared a bedroom. And Frank led him upstairs, shocked by his exhausted appearance and ashy paleness. He patted him on the shoulder, promising to help him; but now he must go to bed—to-morrow they would see what could be done.

When Bertie found himself alone he looked about him. The room was very comfortable; the bed ample, soft, and warm. He felt himself squalid and dirty, amid such surroundings of luxury; and by a natural instinct of decency and cleanliness, though his teeth were chattering with cold, he first carefully and elaborately washed himself—lathering, rubbing, brushing—till his whole body was rosy and glowing, and smelling of soapsuds. He looked in the glass, and only regretted that he had no razors; he would have shaved. At last, having slipped on a nightshirt which lay ready for use, he crept in between the blankets. He did not immediately fall asleep, reveling in the comfort, in his own purification, in the whiteness of the sheets, the warmth of the quilt; in the gleam of the nightlight even, which showed discreetly through a green shade. A smile came into his eyes and parted his lips—and he was asleep; without a thought of the morrow. Happy in the respite of to-day, and the warmth of the bed, his mind almost vacant, indeed, but for the single recurring thought that Frank was really a good fellow!

Fate

CHAPTER II

NEXT morning there was a hard frost; the snow glittered like crystals. They had breakfasted, and Bertie was relating his disasters in America. He had been trimmed and shaved by Frank's barber, and he was wearing Frank's clothes, which were "a world too wide" for him, and a pair of slippers in which his feet were lost. He already felt more at home and began to bask, like a cat which has found a warm spot of sunshine. He lounged at his ease in the armchair, smoking comfortably, and was on the old familiar terms with Frank. His voice was soft and mellow, with a ring of full content, like an alloy of gold. Westhove was interested, and let him tell his story in his own way; and he did so very simply, without making any secret of his poverty; but everything had happened inevitably, and could not have turned out otherwise. He was no favorite of fortune, that was all. But he was tough; many another would not have pulled through as he had.

Frank looked at him in astonishment; he was so frail, so pale, so delicate, almost devoid of all manly development; he was lost in the grotesque amplitude of Frank's coat and trousers—a mere stripling as compared with his own stalwart, angular frame! And he had gone through days of hunger, nights without a shelter, a depth of poverty which to Frank—well fed and ruddy with vigorous health—seemed unendurable; and he spoke of it so coolly, almost jestingly; without complaining, only looking with regretful pity at his hands, which were thin, and blue with the biting cold, and chapped and raw about the knuckles. At the moment the state of his hands seemed to be the only thing that troubled him. A very happy nature, thought Frank, while he laughed at him for his concern about his hands.

But Bertie himself was shocked at his own heedlessness, for he suddenly exclaimed:

"But what am I to do—what am I to do?"

He gazed into vacancy, helpless and desperate, wringing his hands. Frank laughed him out of his despair, poured him out a glass of sherry, and told him that for the present he must stay where he was, to recover. He himself would be heartily glad of Bertie's company for a few weeks; he was a little sick of his wealthy bachelor life; he belonged to a circle of idlers, who went out a great deal, and spent a great deal, and he was tired of it all—dinners and balls in the world, and suppers and orgies in the half-world. It was always the same thing; a life like a *Montagne Russe,* down and then up again, down and then up again, without a moment for thought; an existence made for you, in the position you made for yourself. At the moment he had but one anxiety; Bertie himself. Frank would help him, after a few weeks' rest, to find an appointment, or some employment; but, above all, he was not to worry himself for the present. Westhove was glad to have his old friend under his roof. Memories rose up before him like dissolving views, pale-hued and swift, but appealing to his sympathy—memories of his school-days, of boyish mischief, zigzag excursions, picnics among the sand-hills near The Hague—did Bertie remember? Frank could see him still, the slight, fragile lad, bullied by louts, protected by himself—Frank—whose fists were always ready to hit out, right and left, in defense of his friend. And, later on, their student days in Delft; Bertie's sudden disappearance without leaving a trace, even for Frank; then a few letters at rare intervals, and then years of silence. Oh! he was glad indeed to see his friend at his side once more; he had always had a great love for Bertie, just because Bertie was so wholly unlike himself, with something of the cat about him—loving to be petted and made much of, but now and then irresistibly prompted to flee over roofs and gutters, to get miry and dirty, and return at last to warm and clean himself on the hearth. Frank loved his

Fate

friend as a twin-brother quite different from himself, imposed upon by Bertie's supercilious and delicately egoistic fascination—a catlike creature altogether.

Bertie found it a great luxury to stay indoors the whole of that day, sitting by the fire, which he kept blazing by feeding it with logs. Frank had some capital port, and they sat after lunch sipping it, dreaming or talking; Bertie telling a hundred tales of his adventures in America, of his farmer master, of his hotel, and the theatre where he had acted; and one anecdote led to another, all garnished with a touch of singular romance. Frank presently wanted a little fresh air, and said he would go to his club; but Bertie remained where he was; he could not go about in rags, and he could not appear anywhere with Frank in the clothes he had on. Frank was to return to dinner at eight o'clock. And then suddenly, as if it had come to him like a lightning flash, Bertie said:

"Say nothing about me, pray, to any of your friends. They need not be told that you know such a bad lot as I am. Promise me."

Frank promised, laughing; and, holding out his hand, the "bad lot" added:

"How can I ever repay you? What a happy thing for me that I should have met you! You are the most generous fellow I ever knew!"

Frank escaped from this volley of gratitude, and

Fate

Bertie remained alone in front of the hearth, toasting all over in the blaze, or stretching his legs, with his feet on the shining bars. He poured himself out another glass of port, and made himself think of nothing, reveling in the enjoyment of idleness, while he seriously examined his damaged hands, wondering how best to ensure their rapid recovery.

Fate

CHAPTER III

BERTIE had been a month at White-Rose Cottage, and was now hardly recognizable in the young man who sat by Frank's side in a victoria, in an irreproachable fur-lined coat, a fashionable tall hat; both the men wrapped about the knees in a handsome plaid. He now mixed quite at his ease with Frank's other acquaintances, carefully dressed, agreeable, and entertaining, and lisping English with an affected accent, which he thought elegant. He dined with Frank every day at the club, to which he was introduced; criticized game and wines with the most blasé air in the world, and smoked Havanas at two shillings apiece as if they were mere straw. Frank had in his inmost soul the greatest belief in him, and watched him with a smile of secret satisfaction, as he calmly went his own way chatting with men of the world, without ever for a moment feeling shy; and Frank thought the comedy altogether so amusing that he introduced his friend wherever he went.

Winter yielded to a foggy spring; the London season was upon them, and Bertie seemed to find great pleasure in assisting at afternoon teas, and evenings at home; in sitting at a grand dinner between two pairs of fine shoulders, and flirting with each in turn, never dazzled by the glitter of jewels, nor bewildered by the sparkle of champagne; in leaning with languid grace in the stalls or dress circle, his chiseled features full of distinction and lordly repose, a fragrant white flower gleaming in his button-hole, and his opera-glass dangling between his snow-white fingers, as though not one of the ladies was worthy of his inspection. Frank, for lack of occupation, as a man who takes his pleasure where he finds it, had pushed Bertie forward in the world, not merely to help him, but also for the fun of it—a silly amusement, to make a fool of society! Bertie himself had many scruples, and kept note in a pocketbook of everything Frank spent upon him—when times were better he would repay him all—and in a fortnight it had mounted up to a total of some hundred pounds.

Even at home Frank found him amusing. Bertie, who had contrived, by a few kind words, to win the good graces of Annie and her husband, Westhove's valet and butler, turned all the furniture about in whimsical disorder, bought statuettes, palms, and Oriental stuffs, and changed the unsociable aspect of the room into one of artistic comfort, which invited to indolence; a subdued light, wide divans, the atmosphere of an alcove redolent of Egyptian pastils and fine cigarettes, in which thought floated into dreams, and the half-closed eyes rested on the nude figures of bronze nymphs seen through the greenery of plants. Here, in the evening, high festivals were held; orgies with a few chosen friends, and select fair ones; two ladies from a skating-rink, and a figurante from a theatre, who smoked cigarettes with their vermilion lips and drank to Bertie's health. Frank laughed to his heart's content to see Bertie, a contemner of the fair sex, quite insensible to the three charmers; making game of them, teasing them, setting them by the ears till they were almost ready to claw each other, and, to conclude the matter, pouring floods of champagne down their *décolletés* throats.

No; Frank had never been so well amused during all his long residence in London, where he had settled as an engineer in order to give —as he said—a cosmopolitan character to his knowledge of the world.

He was thoroughly good-hearted, and too highly prosperous to be a deep thinker. He had tasted of every pleasure, and had no high opinion of life, which was after all but a farce, lasting, according to statistics, on an average six-and-thirty years. He made small pretense of any philosophical views of existence, beyond a determined avoidance of everything that was not amusing. Now Bertie was very amusing, not only in his fun with

Fate

women, the cruel sport of a panther; but especially in the farcical part he played in Frank's world, where he figured as a man of fashion—he, a vagabond, who only a month since had stood shivering in rags on the pavement. It was a constant secret delight to his friend, who gave Bertie *carte blanche* to enable him to keep it up; a *carte blanche* which was amply honored, bringing in heavy tailors' bills—for Bertie dressed with refined vanity, bought ties by the dozen, adopted every fancy that came into fashion, and scented himself with all the waters of Rimmel. It was as though he were fain to plunge into every extravagant refinement of an exquisite, after having been a squalid scarecrow. And although at first he kept faithful record of his outlay, he soon forgot first one item and then another, till at last he forgot all.

Thus weeks slipped by, and Frank never thought of troubling himself to inquire among his influential acquaintances for employment for his companion. Their life as wealthy idlers filled their minds entirely; Frank's at any rate, for Bertie had brought a new charm into it.

But suddenly a strange thing happened. One day Bertie went out in the morning alone, and did not come in to lunch. After luncheon, at the club, no Bertie, nor yet at dinner. He did not come home in the evening; he had left no clue. Frank, extremely uneasy, sat up half the night—

no one. Two days went by—still no one. Frank inquired right and left, and at last gave information to the police.

At last one morning, before Frank was up, Bertie appeared at his bedside with an apologetic smile; Frank must not be angry with him; he surely had not been alarmed? You see such a monotonously genteel life had suddenly been too much for him. Always these elegant ladies, with trains and diamonds; always clubs full of lords and baronets; and skating-rinks—the pink of finery! Always a chimney-pot hat, and every evening full dress, with the regulation buttonholer. It was intolerable! He could endure it no longer; it had been too much for him

"But where did you hide yourself?" asked Frank, in utter amazement.

"Oh, here and there, among old acquaintances, I have not been out of London."

"And you did not know a soul here?"

"Oh, well, no fashionable folk, like your friends, but a scapegrace or two. You are not vexed with me?"

Frank had sat up in bed to talk to him. He saw that he looked pale, weary, and unkempt. His trousers were deeply bordered with mud; his hat crushed; there was a three-cornered rent in his greatcoat. And he stood there in evident confusion, like a boy, with his doubting, coaxing smile.

Fate

"Come, do not be cross with me; take me into favor once more."

This was too much for Frank. Provoked beyond measure, he exclaimed:

"But, Bertie, what a cad you look! And where on earth have you been?" he asked again.

"Oh, here and there."

And he could get no more out of him. Bertie would only say that he had wanted to disappear; and now he was tired—he would go to bed. He slept till three in the afternoon. Frank laughed over it all day, and Bertie went into fits when he heard of the police. At dinner, at the club, he related, with a melancholy face, that he had been out of town for a few days, attending a funeral. Frank had failed to receive a note through the carelessness of a servant.

"But where in the world have you really been?" whispered Frank for the third time, infinitely amused and inquisitive.

"Here and there, I tell you—first in one place, and then in another," answered Bertie, with the most innocent face in the world; and, dapper as ever, he delicately lifted an oyster, his little finger in the air, and swallowed down his half dozen without another word on the subject.

Fate

CHAPTER IV

THE season passed away, but Bertie remained. Sometimes, indeed, he talked of going to Holland; he had an uncle, a stockbroker, in Amsterdam. Possibly that uncle— But Westhove would not hear of it; and, when his friend's conscience pricked him for sponging on him, he talked him down. What did it matter? If Bertie had been the rich man, and he the pauper, Bertie would have done the same by him. They were friends.

A true appreciation of the case began to dawn on him in the now firmly established habits of their life. Frank's moral sense whispered drowsily in the ease of their luxurious existence. Now and then, indeed, he had something like a vague suspicion that he was not rich enough for two; that he had spent more in the last few months than in any former season. But he was too heedless to dwell long on such unpleasant doubts. He was lulled to sleep by Bertie as if by opium or morphia. Bertie had become indispensable to him: he consulted his friend on every point, and allowed himself to be led by him on every occasion, completely

Fate

subjugated by the ascendency held over him by the fragile little man, with his velvet paws, as though he had him under a yoke. Every now and then—erelong at frequent intervals of about a fortnight —Bertie disappeared, stayed away four or five days, and came back one fine morning, with his insinuating smile, exhausted, pale, and tired out. These were, perhaps, some secret excesses of dissipation—mysterious adventure-hunting in the sordid purlieus of the lowest neighborhoods—of which Frank never heard nor understood the truth; a depth of depravity into which Frank seemed too precise and dainty to be initiated; sins in which he was to have no part, and which Bertie, in his refinement of selfishness, kept for himself as an occasional treat.

Then Frank's hours were passed in disgust of life; he missed the unwholesome stimulant of his existence; in his solitude he sank into gray melancholy and sadness, verging on despair. He stayed at home all day, incapable of any exertion, sulking in his lonely house, where everything—the draping of the handsome curtains, the bronze nudity of the statues, the careless disarray of the cushions on the divan—had still, as it were, an odor of Bertie, which haunted him with regret. On such days as these he was conscious of the futility of his existence, the odious insignificance of his sinewless, empty life: useless, aimless, null!

Fate

Sadly sweet memories would come over him; reminiscences of his parental home, shining through the magic glass of retrospect like bright, still pools of tender domestic harmony, in which the figures of his father and mother stood forth grand and noble, glorified by childlike affection. He longed for some unspeakable ideal, something pure and chaste, some high aim in life. He would shake off this torpor of the soul; he would send away Bertie—

But Bertie came back, and Bertie held him tightly once more in his silken bonds, and he saw more clearly every day that he could not live without Bertie. And then, catching sight of himself in a mirror—tall and brawny and strong, the healthy blood tinging his clear complexion—he could not forbear smiling at the foolish visions of his solitude, which struck him now as diseased imaginings, quite out of keeping with his robust vigor. Life was but a farce, and the better part was to play it out as a farce, in mere sensual enjoyment. Nothing else was worth the pains— And yet sometimes at night, when his big body lay tired out after some riotous evening, a gnawing dissatisfaction would come over him, not to be conquered by this light-hearted philosophy, and even Bertie himself would lecture him. Why did not Frank seek some employment—some sphere of action? Why did not he travel for awhile?

Fate

"Why not go to Norway?" asked Bertie one day, for the sake of saying something.

London was beginning to be intolerable to Bertie; and as the notion of traveling smiled on Frank, both for a change and for economy—since they could live more cheaply abroad than in the whirl of fashionable London—he thought it over, and came to a decision to leave White-Rose Cottage for an indefinite period to the care of Annie and her husband, and spend a few weeks in Norway. Bertie should go with him.

Fate

CHAPTER V

AFTER luncheon at the *table d'hôte* of the Britannia Hotel at Trondhjem, the friends made their way along the broad, quiet streets with their low, wooden houses, and they had left the town, going in the direction of the Gjeitfjeld, when they overtook, in the village of Ihlen, an elderly gentleman with a young girl, evidently bent on the same excursion. The pair had sat a few places off at the *table d'hôte*, and as this much acquaintance justified a recognition in so lonely a spot, Westhove and his friend lifted their hats. The old gentleman immediately asked, in English, whether they knew the road to the Gjeitfjeld: he and his daughter—who, during the colloquy, never looked up from her "Baedeker"—could not agree on the subject. This difference of opinion led to a conversation: the two young men begged to be allowed to join them, Frank being of opinion that "Baedeker" was right.

"Papa will never believe in 'Baedeker!'" said the young lady with a quiet smile, as she closed the red volume she had been consulting. "Nor

27

will he ever trust me when I tell him I will guide him safely."

"Are you always so sure of knowing your way?" said Frank, laughing.

"Always!" she saucily declared, with a gay laugh.

Bertie inquired how long a walk it was, and what was to be seen at the end of it; Frank's everlasting walks were a weariness and a bore. During his residence with his friend he had so spoiled himself, in order to forget his former wretchedness, that he now knew no greater pleasure than that of lying on a bench with a cigar, or a glass of port, and, above all, would avoid every exertion. But now, abroad—when a man is traveling—he can not forever sit dozing in his hotel. Besides, he was quite stiff with riding in a cariole; all this useless rushing about was really monstrous folly, and White-Rose Cottage was not such a bad place. Frank, on the contrary, thoroughly enjoyed the clear, invigorating air of this brilliant summer day, and he drank in the sunshine as though it were fine wine cooled by a fresh mountain breeze; his step was elastic and his voice had a contented ring.

"Are you an Englishman?" asked the gentleman.

Westhove explained that they were Dutch, that they lived in London; and his tone had the frank

Fate

briskness which a man instinctively adopts to fellow-travelers, as sharing his lot for the moment, when the weather is fine and the landscape pleasing. Their sympathy being thus aroused by their admiration of Norwegian scenery, they walked on side by side, the elder man stepping out bravely, the young lady very erect, with her fine figure molded in a simple, close-fitting blue cloth dress, to which a cape with several folds—something like an elegant type of coachman's cape—lent a dash of smartness. She wore a sort of jockey-cap, with a mannish air, on her thick twists of ruddy-gold hair.

Bertie alone could not understand how all this could be called pleasure; but he made no complaint. He spoke little, not thinking it necessary to make himself agreeable to people whom he might probably never set eyes on again after the morrow. So he just kept up with them, wondering at Frank, who had at once plunged into eager conversation with the young lady, but perceiving on a sudden that his own politeness and tact were a mere superficial varnish as compared with Frank's instinctive good breeding. At that moment, for the first time, notwithstanding his better features and natty traveling costume, he felt himself so far Frank's inferior that a surge of fury resembling hate thrilled through him. He could not bear this sense of inferiority, so he approached the old gentleman, and, walking by his side, forced himself to a show of respectful amiability. As they followed the windings of the upward and diminishing path they by degrees lagged behind Frank and his companion, and thus climbed the hill two and two.

"So you live in London. What is your name?" asked the young lady, with calm curiosity.

"Frank Westhove."

"My name is Eva Rhodes; my father is Sir Archibald Rhodes, of Rhodes Grove. And your friend?"

"His name is Robert van Maeren."

"I like the sound of your name best. I believe I can say it like English. Tell it me again."

He repeated his name, and she said it after him with her English accent. It was very funny, and they laughed over it—"Fraank. Fraank Westhoove."

And then they looked back.

"Papa, are you tired?" cried Eva. The old man was toiling up the height with his broad shoulders bent; his face was red under his traveling cap, which he had pushed to the back of his head, and he was blowing like a Triton. Bertie tried to smile pleasantly, though he was inwardly raging in high dudgeon over this senseless clamber. They had half an hour more of it, however, before the narrow track, which zigzagged up the hill-side

Fate

like a gray arabesque, came to an end, and they sat down to rest on a block of stone.

Eva was enchanted. Far below lay Trondhjem with its modern houses, encircled by the steely waters of the Nid and its fjord, a magic mirror on which floated the white mass of the fortress of Munkenholm. The mountains rising on all sides were blue; nearest to them the bloomy, purple blue of the grape; then the deep sheeny blue of velvet; farther off the transparent, crystalline blue of the sapphire, and in the distance the tender sky-blue of the turquoise. The water was blue, like blue silver; the very air was blue as pearls are or mother-of-pearls. The equable sunlight fell on everything, without glare and without shadow, from exactly overhead.

"It is almost like Italy!" exclaimed Eva. "And this is Norway! I had always pictured Norway to myself as being all like Romsdal, wild and barren, with rocky peaks like the Romsdalhorn and the Trolltinder, and with raging cascades like the Sletta fos; but this is quite lovely, and so softly blue! I should like to build a house here and live in it, and I would call it Eva's Bower, and keep a whole flock of white doves; they would look so pretty flying in the blue air."

"Dear child!" laughed Sir Archibald. "It looks very different in winter, I suspect."

"No doubt different, but still lovely. In winter

Fate

I should love the fury of raging winds, and the roar of the waves of the fjord below my house, and gray mists would hang over the hills! I can see it all!"

"Why, you would be frozen," argued the father, gravely.

"Oh, no; and I should sit at my turret window, dreaming over Dante or Spenser. Do you love Dante and Spenser?"

The question was addressed to Frank, who had listened somewhat puzzled to Eva's raptures, and was now a little startled; for, you see, though he knew Dante by name, he had never even heard of the poet Spenser; only of Herbert Spencer.

"What, do you not know the Faery Queen, Una, and the Red-cross Knight, and Britomart? How very strange!"

"Dear child, what a little fanatic you are over those silly allegories!" said papa.

"But they are glorious, papa!" Eva insisted. "Besides, I love allegory above all things, and admire no other kind of poetry."

"The style is so affected! You are drowned in symbolism!"

"It is the keynote of the Renaissance," Eva protested. "In the time of Elizabeth all the Court talked in that high-flown style. And Edmund Spenser's images are splendid; they sparkle like jewels!"

Fate

Bertie thought this discourse much too learned, but he kept his opinion to himself, and made some remark about Dante's "Inferno." They were by this time rested and went on again up the hill.

"My daughter is half an 'Esthetic,'" said the old gentleman, laughing. And Eva laughed too.

"Nay. That is not the truth, papa. Do not believe him, Mr.—Mr. Westhove. Do you know what makes papa say so? A few years ago, when I had but just left school, I and a few girls I knew were perfectly idiotic for a while. We tousled our hair into mops, dressed in floppy garments of damask and brocade with enormous sleeves, and held meetings among ourselves to talk nonsense about art. We sat in attitudes, holding a sunflower or a peacock's feather, and were perfectly ridiculous. That is why papa still says such things. I am not so silly now. But I am still very fond of reading; and is that so very esthetic?"

Frank looked smilingly into her honest, clear, gray eyes, and her ringing, decided voice had an apologetic tone, as if she were asking pardon for her little display of learning. He understood that there was nothing of the blue-stocking in this girl, as might have seemed from her sententious jest before, and he was quite vexed with himself for having been compelled to confess that he knew nothing of the poet Spenser. How stupid she must think him!

Fate

But it was a moment when the beauties of the scenery had so bewitched them that they moved, as it were, in a magic circle of sympathy, in which some unknown law overruled their natural impulses, something electrically swift and ethereally subtle.

As they climbed the meandering mountain track, or made short cuts through the low brushwood, where the leaves glistened in the sun like polished green needles, and as he breathed that pure, intoxicating air, Frank felt as though he had known her quite a long time, as if it were years since he had first seen her at the *table d'hôte* at Trondhjem. And Sir Archibald and Bertie, lingering behind, were far off—miles away—mere remembered images. Eva's voice joined with his own in harmonious union, as though their fragmentary talk of art and poetry were a duet which they both knew how to sing, although Frank candidly confessed that he had read but little, and that what he had read he scarcely remembered. She playfully scolded him, and her sweet clear tones now and then startled a bird, which flew piping out of the shrubs. He felt within him a revival of strength—a new birth; and would fain have spread his arms to embrace —the air!

Fate

CHAPTER VI

THAT evening, on their return from their walk, after dinner, over a cup of coffee, they discussed their further projects.

"We are going to Molde," said Sir Archibald.

"And so are we!" Frank exclaimed.

The old gentleman at once expressed a wish that the friends would continue to give him and his daughter the pleasure of their society. Frank had taken a great fancy to him, and Bertie thought him courteous, and good company; Bertie had talked a good deal about America, but he had not told the whole history of his farming experiences in the far West; he had indeed idealized it a little by speaking of "my farm." And Frank did not contradict him.

By the end of two days spent at Trondhjem they were the best of friends; with that confidential intimacy which, on a tour, when etiquette is out of court, sometimes arises from mere contact, without any knowledge of character on either side, simply from sympathy in trifles and mutual attraction, a superficial sentiment of transient admira-

Fate

tion which occupies the traveler's leisure. The day on the sea by steamboat to Molde was like a party of pleasure, in spite of the rain which drove them below; and in the cabin, over a bottle of champagne, Miss Eva and the three men played a rubber of whist. But afterward, in a gleam of pale sunshine, there was an endless walk to and fro on the wet deck. The low rocky shore glided slowly past on the larboard side; the hills, varying in outline—now close together, and again showing a gap—covered with brown moss down by the water, and gray above with patches of pale rose or dull purple light. At Christiansand they were far from land, and the waters, now rougher, were crimson in the glory of the sinking sun, fast approaching the horizon. Every wave had a crest of flame-colored foam, as though the ocean were on fire. Frank and Eva, meanwhile, pacing up and down, laughed at each other's faces, reddened like a couple of peonies, or like two maskers rouged by the glow of the sun to the semblance of clowns.

They reached Molde late at night, too late to see its lovely fjord. But next morning, there it lay before them, a long, narrow inlet, encircled by mountains capped with snow; a poem, a song of mountains; pure, lofty, beautiful, severe, solemn, without one jarring note. The sky above them was calmly gray, like brooding melancholy, and

Fate

the peace that reigned sounded like a passionless *andante*.

Next day, when Sir Archibald proposed a walk up Moldehoï, Bertie declared that he was tired, and did not feel well, and begged to be left at home. In point of fact, he thought that the weather did not look promising; heavy clouds were gathering about the chain of hill-tops which shut in the fjord, like a sweeping drapery of rain, threatening erelong to fall and wrap everything in their gloomy folds. Eva, however, would not be checked by bad weather: when people were traveling they must not be afraid of a wetting. So the three set out; and Bertie, in his patent slippers, remained in the drawing-room of the Grand Hotel, with a book and a half-pint bottle.

The road was muddy, but they stepped out valiantly in their waterproofs and stout boots. The rain which hung threateningly above their heads did not daunt them, but gave a touch of romantic adventure to the expedition, as though it threatened to submerge them in an impending deluge. Once off the beaten road, and still toiling upward, they occasionally missed the track, which was lost in a plashy bog, or under ferns dripping with rain, or struck across a wild growth of blue bilberries. They crossed the morass, using the rocks as stepping-stones; the old gentleman without help, and Eva with her hand in Frank's, fearing lest her little feet should slide on the smooth green moss. She laughed gaily, skipping from stone to stone with his help; sometimes suddenly slipping and supporting herself against his shoulder, and then again going on bravely, trying the stones with her stout stick. She felt as though she need take no particular heed, now that he was at her side; that he would support her if she stumbled; and they chatted eagerly as they went, almost leaping from rock to rock.

"What sort of man is your friend, Mr. Westhove?" Eva suddenly inquired.

Frank was a little startled; it was always an unpleasant task to give any information concerning Bertie, less on account of his past life than of his present position, his quiet sponging on himself, Frank, who, though enslaved by Bertie, knew full well that the situation was strange, to say the least of it, in the eyes of the world.

"Oh he is a man who has been very unfortunate," he said evasively, and he presently added: "Has he not made a pleasant impression on you?"

Eva laughed so heartily that she was near falling into a pool of mud, if Frank had not firmly thrown his arm round her waist.

"Eva, Eva!" cried her father, shaking his head, "pray be more careful!"

Eva drew herself up with a slight blush.

Fate

"What can I say?" she went on, pursuing the subject. "If I were to speak the whole truth—"

"Of course."

"But perhaps you will be vexed; for I can see very plainly that you are quite infatuated with your friend."

"Then you do not like him?"

"Well, then, if you insist on knowing, the first day, when I made his acquaintance, I thought him insufferable. With you we got on famously at once, as an amusing traveling companion, but with him—but perhaps he has not traveled much?"

"Oh, yes, he has," said Frank, who could not help smiling.

"Well, then, perhaps he was shy or awkward. However, I began to think differently of him after that; I don't think him insufferable now."

It was strange, but Frank felt no particular satisfaction on hearing of the young lady's changed opinion; he made no reply.

"You say he has had much to trouble him. And, indeed, I can see it in his face. There is something so gentle in him, so tender, I might almost say; such soft, dark eyes, and such a sweet voice. At first, as I tell you, I found it intolerable, but now it strikes me as rather poetical. He must certainly be a poet, and have been crossed in love: he can be no commonplace man."

"No, that he certainly is not," said Frank,

Fate

vaguely, a little ill at ease over Eva's raptures;
and a mingling of jealousy and regret—something
like an aversion for the worldly polish, and a dull
envy of the poetic graces which Eva attributed to
his friend—ran through his veins like a chill. He
glanced up, almost pathetically, at the pretty
creature, who was sometimes so shrewd and sometimes so naive; so learned in all that bore on her
favorite studies, so ignorant of real life. A dim
compassion came over him, and on a sudden the
gray rain-clouds weighed upon him with a pall of
melancholy, as though they were ominous of some
inevitable fatality which threatened to crush her.
His fingers involuntarily clasped her hand more
tightly.

"Here is the path once more!" cried Sir Archibald, who was twenty steps ahead of them.

"Oh, yes! There is the path! Thank you, Mr.
Westhove!" said Eva, and she sprang from the
last stepping-stone, pushing her way through the
snapping bracken to the beaten track.

"And up there is the hut with the weather-cock,"
her father went on. "I believe we have made a
long round out of our way. Instead of chattering
so much, you would do well to keep a sharp look-
out for the path. My old eyes, you know—"

"But it was great fun jumping over the stones,"
laughed Eva.

Far above them they could now see the hut with

the tall pole of the weather-cock, and they went on at an easier pace, their feet sinking in the violet and pink blossomed heath, crushing the bilberries, dimly purple like tiny grapes. Eva stooped and picked some.

"Oh! so nice and sweet!" she exclaimed, with childish surprise, and she pulled some more, dyeing her lips and fingers blue with the juice of the berries. "Taste them, Mr. Westhove."

He took them from her soft, small hand, stained as it were with purple blood. It was true; they were deliciously sweet, and such fine ones!

And then they went on again, following Sir Archibald, often stopping, and triumphing like children when they came on a large patch where the whortleberries had spread unhindered like a miniature orchard.

"Papa, papa! Do try them!" Eva cried, heedless of the fact that papa was far ahead; but Sir Archibald was not out of sight, and they had to run to overtake him; Eva's laughter ringing like a bell, while she lamented that she must leave so many berries untouched—and such beauties!

"I dare say there will be plenty round the hut," said Frank, consolingly.

"Do you think so?" she said, with a merry laugh. "Oh, what a couple of babies we are!"

The path grew wider, and they found it easy walking up to the top, sometimes quitting the

Fate

track and scrambling over the stones to shorten the way. Presently they heard a shout, and, looking up, they saw Sir Archibald standing on the cairn in which the staff of the weather-cock was fixed, and waving his traveling-cap. They hurried on, and soon were at his side. Eva knocked at the door of the hut.

"The hut is shut up," said her father.

"How stupid!" she exclaimed. "Why does it stand here at all if it is shut up? Does no one live in it?"

"Why, of course not," said Sir Archibald, as if it was the most natural thing in the world.

Frank helped Eva to climb the cairn round the pole, and they looked down on the panorama at their feet.

"It is beautiful, but melancholy," said Eva.

The long fjord lay below them, a narrow ribbon of pale, motionless water, hemmed in by the mountains, now wreathed with gray vapor, through which they gleamed fitfully like ghosts of mountains; Lauparen and Vengetinder, Trolltinder and Romsdalhorn, towering up through the envious, rolling mist, which, swelled by the coming storm, hung in black clouds from every peak and cast a gloomy reflection on the still waters. The hills were weeping—unsubstantial, motionless phantoms, sorrowing and tragical under some august and superhuman woe—a grief as of giants and

Fate

demigods; the fjord, with its township, a plot of gardens, and roofs, and walls, and the white châlet of the Grand Hotel—all weeping, all motionless under the gloomy sky. A ghostly chill rose up from the gulf to where the trio stood, mingling with the tangible clamminess of the mist, which seemed to weigh on their eyelids. It was not raining, but the moisture seemed to distil on them from the black unbroken rack of clouds; and to the westward, between two cliffs which parted to show a gleaming strip of ocean, a streak was visible of pale gold and faint rose-color—hardly more than a touch of pink, a sparkle of gold—a stinted alms of the setting sun. They scarcely said another word, oppressed by the superhuman sadness which enwrapped them like a shroud. When Eva at last spoke her clear voice sounded far away—through a curtain.

"Look, there is a glint of sunshine over the sea. Here we are pining for the sun. Oh, I wish the sun would break through the clouds! It is so dismal here—so dreary! How well I understand Oswald's cry in Ibsen's 'Ghosts' when he is going mad: 'The sun, the sun!' Men might pray for sunshine here and get no more than that distant gleam. Oh, I am perished!"

She shivered violently under the stiff, shining folds of her waterproof cloak; her face was drawn and white, and her eyes looked large and anxious.

Fate

She suddenly felt herself so forlorn and lonely
that she instinctively took her father's arm and
clung to him closely.

"Are you cold, my child; shall we go home?"
he asked.

She nodded, and they both helped her down the
heap of stones. Why, she knew not, but suddenly
she had thought of her mother, who was dead, and
wondered whether she had ever felt thus forlorn
in spite of her father's fondness. But when they
came in sight of the hut again, she said, as if it had
just occurred to her:

"Papa, there are some names cut in the door;
let us cut ours too."

"But, child, you are so cold and pale—"

"Never mind; let us cut our names; I want
to," she urged, like a spoiled child.

"No, Eva—what nonsense!"

"Oh, but I do want to," she repeated coaxingly,
but the old man would not give in, grumbling
still; Frank, however, pulled out his pocket-knife.

"Oh, Mr. Westhove, do cut my name; nothing
but Eva—only three letters. Will you?" she asked
softly.

Frank had it on his lips to say that he would
like to cut his own name with hers, although it
was so long, but he was silent; it would have
sounded flat and commonplace in the midst of
this mournful scenery. So he carved the letters

on the door, which was like a traveler's album. Eva stood gazing out to the west, and she saw the three streaks of gold turn pale, and the rose-tint fade away.

"The sun, the sun!" she murmured, with a shudder, and a faint smile on her white lips and in her tearful eyes.

A few heavy drops of rain had begun to fall. Sir Archibald asked if they were ever coming, and led the way. Eva nodded with a smile, and went up to Frank:

"Have you done it, Mr. Westhove?"

"Yes," said Frank, hastily finishing the last letter.

She looked up, and saw that he had cut "Eva Rhodes," and in very neat, even letters, smoothly finished. Below he had roughly cut "Frank," in a great hurry.

"Why did you add 'Rhodes'?" she asked, and her voice was faint, as if far away.

"Because it took longer," Frank replied simply.

Fate

CHAPTER VII

THEY got back to the Grand Hotel in a torrent
of rain, a deluge poured out of all the urns of
heaven; muddy to their waists, wet to the skin,
and chilled to the bone. Eva, after a hot supper,
was sent off to bed by her father, and the three
men—Sir Archibald, Frank, and Bertie—sat in
the drawing-room, where a few other visitors, all
very cross at the bad weather, tried to solace themselves with illustrated papers or albums. The old
gentleman took a doze in an easy-chair. Frank
gazed pensively at the straight streaks of rain,
which fell like an endless curtain of close steel
needles, thrashing the surface of the fjord. Bertie
sipped a hot grog, and looked at his shiny slippers.

"And did you not miss my company on your
excursion?" he asked, addressing Frank with a
smile, just to break the silence that reigned in the
room.

Westhove turned to him in some surprise, as if
roused from a dream; then, with a frank laugh,
he briefly answered:

"No."

Bertie stared at him, but his friend had already

turned away, lost in thought over the patter of the rain; so Bertie at last took up his book again, and tried to read. But the letters danced before his eyes; his ears and nerves still thrilled uncomfortably under the remembrance of that one short, astounding word which Frank had fired into the silence like a leaden bullet. It annoyed him that Frank should take no further notice of him.

Frank stood unmoved, looking out at the mountains, scarcely visible through the watery shroud; what he saw was their walk back from Moldehoï; the meandering downward path through the tall, dripping bracken; the pelting rain streaming in their faces as from a watering-pot; Eva, closely wrapped in her wet mackintosh, and clinging to his arm as if seeking his protection; behind them her father, carefully feeling the slippery, moss-grown stones with his walking-stick. Frank had wanted to wrap her in his own thick waterproof coat, but this she had positively rejected; she would not have him made ill for her sake, she said, in that far-away voice. And then, when they were at home again, after they had changed their clothes and dined, and laughed over their adventure, Sir Archibald was afraid lest Eva should have taken cold.

Frank remembered at this moment a fragment of their conversation; his asking her, a little surprised in spite of himself, "Have you read Ibsen's

Fate

'Ghosts'? You spoke of Oswald when we were up on Moldehoï."

As it happened, he had himself read "Ghosts," and he did not think it a book for a young girl; she had noticed his surprise, and had blushed deeply as she replied:

"Yes, I have read it. I read a great deal, and papa has brought me up on rather liberal lines. Do you think that I ought not to have read 'Ghosts'?"

She herself had seen no harm in it, had not perhaps fully understood it, as she candidly confessed. He had not ventured to tell her that the study of such a drama of physiological heredity was, to say the least, unnecessary for a young girl; he had answered vaguely, and she had colored yet more deeply, and said no more.

"She must have regarded me as a prig of a schoolmaster!" thought he, ill at ease. "Why should she not read what she likes? She does not need my permission for her reading; she is grown up enough. She must have thought me a pedantic owl."

"Frank!" said Bertie again.

"What?" said Frank, startled.

"We leave this place to-morrow morning, I suppose?'

"Yes, that was our plan. At least if the weather improves."

Fate

"What is the name of the next outlandish spot we are going to?"

"Veblungsnaes; and from thence to Romsdal and Gudbrandsdal."

"And the Rhodeses?"

"They are going to Bergen."

"To-morrow?"

"I don't know."

And he stood once more lost in thought; the gray, wet atmosphere without cast a gloom on the scene within; and in his soul, too, reigned the deepest gloom. What was the use of fostering warm feelings when a few days of sympathetic companionship could only end in parting? This was always the case with friendly traveling acquaintance, and was it not so throughout life, with every one—everything—we love? Was it worth while to care for anything? Was not all love a great delusion, by which men blinded themselves to their disgust with life?

Fate

CHAPTER VIII

DECEMBER in London. Cold and foggy. White-Rose Cottage wrapped in mist; in the back room a blazing fire.

But Robert van Maeren was no longer in the blissful mood to enjoy this luxury, as we have hitherto known him; moreover, he now regarded it as quite a matter of course, which came to him by right, since he was a creature of such refined feeling, so slight and fragile, and did not feel himself born to endure poverty and want. Still, he had known misery, the slavery of hired labor, to which he had bent his back with crafty subservience; still, he had felt the gnawings of hunger, the bitterness of squalid beggary. But all this seemed long ago, and as vague as a dream, or as the vanishing lines of the London streets out there, dimmed and blurred by the pall of fog; as indistinct as our dubious impressions of a former state of existence. For, after his metamorphosis, he had determined to forget—he had forced himself to forget; never for an instant to recall his sufferings, or to think of the future. He hated the past as an injustice, a disgrace, an ineradicable

Fate

stain on the superficial spotlessness of his present
life; he had persuaded himself that all those things
which he had now hidden, buried, forever ignored, had indeed never happened. And he had
succeeded in this effacement of his life in America; it seemed wiped out of the annals of his
memory.

Why, now, must those years rise slowly before
him, like ghosts out of the grave of oblivion?
What had they to say to him now? Nearer and
nearer, till, year by year, month by month, day by
day, they passed before him, dancing in the flames
at which he sat staring, like a dance of death of
the years. They grinned at him from skulls, with
hollow eyes and pallid faces, distorted by a crafty
smile; the dead years which beckoned to him,
wearing filthy rags, and poisoning his cigar with
their foul odor! He saw them, he smelt them; he
shuddered with their chill—there, in front of the
fire; he felt their hunger, in spite of the dinner
that awaited him. Why was it that the future,
which he no less persistently ignored, was beginning to hang over him as an omen of evil, which
each day, each hour, brought nearer and nearer
irresistibly, inevitably?

That future must perhaps be such as the past
had been.

Yes, something was impending. There he sat,
sick with alarms, cowardly, spiritless, effete.

Fate

Something was in the air; he felt it coming nearer, to overwhelm him, to wrestle with him for life or death in a frenzy of despair; he felt himself tottering, sinking; he was torn from the ease and comfort of his present life, cast out into the streets, without shelter, without anything! For what had he of his own? The clothes he wore, the shoes on his feet, the ring on his finger were Frank's. The dinner to come, the bed upstairs, were Frank's. Thus had it been for a year past; and if he were to go with all he possessed, he would go—naked, in the winter.

And he could not again be as he had been in America, tramping for work day after day. His body and mind alike were enervated, as by a warm bath of luxury; he had become like a hot-house plant which is accustomed to the moist heat, and perishes when it is placed in the open air. But it hung over him, cruel and unrelenting; not for an instant did the threat relax, and in his abject weakness he feebly wrung his white hands, and two tears, hot with despair, rolled down his cheeks.

Struggle for existence! He was incapable of such a battle; his energy was too lax for that— a laxity which he had felt growing on him as a joy after his fight for life, but which now had made him powerless to screw himself up to the merest semblance of determination.

Fate

And before him he saw the fateful chain of events passing onward—some so infinitely small —each detail a terrible link, and all leading on to catastrophe. Strange that each one was the outcome of its predecessor! the future the outcome of the past! If, after his failure from sheer idleness at Leyden, his father had not placed him as clerk in the office of a Manchester house, he would probably never have known certain youths, his fellow clerks, fashionable young rakes, and fierce "strugglers for existence"; still scarcely more than boys, and already the worse for dissipation. If he had never known them—and yet, how pleasantly had they borne him along, merely by humoring his natural bent!—he might, perhaps, not have played such underhand tricks with the money belonging to the firm, that his patron, out of sympathy and regard for his father, had shipped him off to America. That was where he had sunk deepest, swamped in the maelstrom of more energetic fortune-hunters. If only he had been less unlucky in America, he would not have found himself stranded in London in such utter destitution, or have appealed to Westhove for help.

And Frank—but for his suggestion, Frank would never have gone to Norway, never have met Eva. Oh, that journey to Norway! how he cursed it now; for Frank might, perhaps, not have fallen in love, and never have thought of mar-

Fate

riage. And now—only yesterday Westhove had called at Sir Archibald's house, where the two friends had been made very welcome after their acquaintance in Norway, and had come home engaged to Eva. Frank would marry, and he, Bertie? Where was he to go? What was to become of him?

He was painfully conscious of the fatality of life, of the injustice of the dispensations of fortune; and he discerned that his own immediate difficulties owed their origin to a single word. One single word: Norway!—Norway, Eva, Frank's falling in love, Frank's engagement and marriage, and his own shipwreck—how horribly clearly he saw every link of the chain of his own life in each word! One word, uttered under a foolish impulse: Norway! And it had irretrievably wrought the happiness of two other persons at the cost of his own. Injustice! Injustice!

And he cursed the impulse, the mysterious, innate force which more or less prompts every word we speak; and he cursed the fact that every word uttered by the tongue of man remains beyond recall. What is that impulse? Something obscurely good, an unconscious "better self," as men declare, which, though deeply and mysteriously hidden, dashes ahead like an unbroken colt, treading down the most elaborate results of careful thought? Oh, if he had but held his tongue! Why Norway?

Fate

What concern had he with that one fatal, fateful land, above all others? Why not Spain, Russia, Japan, good God! Kamchatka, for aught he cared; why especially Norway? Idiotic impulse, which had unlocked his miserable lips to pronounce that luckless name; and oh, the injustice of fate, of life, of everything!

Energy? Will? What could will and energy do against Fate? They were words, empty words. Be a cringing fatalist, like a Turk or Arab, and let day follow day; never think, for behind thought lurks impulse! Fight? Against Fate, who forges her chains blindly, though surely, link upon link?

He threw himself back in his chair, still feebly wringing his hands, and the tears trickled again and again down his cheeks. He saw his own cowardice take shape before him; he stared into its frightened eyes, and he did not condemn it. For he was as Fate had made him. He was a craven, and he could not help it. Men called such a one as he a coward: it was but a word. Why coward, or simple and loyal and brave, or good and noble? It was all a matter of convention, of accepted meaning; the whole world was mere convention, a concept, an illusion of the brain.

There was nothing real at all—nothing!

And yet there was something real: misery and

Fate

poverty were real. He had felt them, wrestled with them hand to hand; and now he was too weak to fight them again, too delicate, too refined! He *would* not face them again. Then, leaning back with his pallid head resting against the cushioned back of his chair, his deep-set black eyes clouded with the venom of these reflections, he was aware of a gentle, pleasant electric current thrilling through him—a current of Will. Fatality had willed to bring Frank and Eva together; well, he—a mere plaything of fate—would will, that—

Yes. He would will to part them.

And before his very eyes, as it seemed, that purpose rose up, cold and rigid, an evil and mysterious form, like an incarnation of Satanic malignity.

It looked at him with the eye of a Sibyl, of a Sphinx; and, as compared with the Titanic cruelty of that image, his former visions sank into nothingness—the Dance of Death of the years, the continuity of Fatality, and his cursing of it all. These now vanished, and he only saw that figure, like a ghost, almost tangible and almost visibly solid in the dusk, against the dying glow of the fire. The gloomy, questioning gaze of those eyes hypnotized his soul; his instinct fell asleep under its crushing power. . . . Friendship! gratitude! They, too, were mere words.

Fate

There was nothing real in life but conventionality and—poverty. And then there was that image —there, in front of the fire—with its staring, fixed gaze, petrified to an embodiment of silent, irresistible, infernal magnetism!

CHAPTER IX

THAT night—he saw Frank no more, for he had stayed to dine with Sir Archibald Rhodes—that night Van Maeren could not sleep; the wildest fancies kept him wide awake. Illusions and schemes whirled through his fevered brain; strange voices buzzed in his ears, hissing like an angry sea.

He saw himself sitting with Eva in a cab, passing through the gloomiest and foulest parts of London. Squalid figures stood in their way, and came close to Eva. He laughed as he saw her dragged away by men with brutal faces, and then come back to him, with her clothes torn, sobbing because she had been insulted. A fearful headache hammered in his brain, and he groaned with a painful effort to control the wild extravagance of his fancy. He got up, rubbing his eyes, as if to drive away the melodramatic vision, and wrapped his burning head in a wet, cold towel. He involuntarily looked in the glass; and, in the subdued glimmer of the nightlight, his face stared back at him as pale as death, drawn and

Fate

haggard, with hollow, sunken eyes, and a gaping mouth. His heart beat violently; as if it were rising into his throat, and he pressed it down with both hands.

After drinking a glass of water he lay down again, forcing himself to be calm. Subtler fancies now crowded his mind, like fine threads caught athwart and across—webs mingled in a maze like an inextricable tangle of lace; and his imagination worked out the intricacies of wearisome intrigues, as though he were a poet who, during a night of lucid sleeplessness, constructs a drama, and, not content with its plot, goes through it again and again, to master the great conception in his mind before writing it out.

Now he saw the orgies of a past day repeating themselves below in the sitting-room. He saw the skating-rink, and Frank and himself drinking champagne, and laughing and singing. But suddenly the door opened, and Sir Archibald came in with Eva on his arm. Sir Archibald cursed Frank with tremendous words and vehement gestures, and Frank hung his head; but Eva threw herself between them, with words of anguish and imploring hands. And it was all the last scene of the fourth act of an opera. The singing in his ears, and the dreadful throbbing in his aching head, were like the thunder of a full orchestra, excited to the utmost by the beat of an energetic conductor, and the loud, strident crash of orass instruments.

Bertie moaned, and tossed from side to side, compelling himself to picture less violent scenes. Now it was like a modern comedy. Eva, at his suggestion, was suspiciously watching Annie, the maid and housekeeper at White-Rose Cottage. Eva was jealous, and then a grand catastrophe— Eva finding Annie in Frank's arms.

Sick with thinking, bewildered by his own imaginings, he drove away the chaotic vision. Exhaustion overcame him; his frenzy was worn out, though his head was still burning, throbbing, bursting; although acute pain shot through his brain, from his brows to his neck, as if he were being scalped; although the blood in his temples leaped furiously in his veins, with rhythmical torture.

And in the immediate torment of physical suffering, his pride, which was to defy Fatality, collapsed like a tower crumbling into ruins. His imagination became vacancy; he forgot his terrors of the future. He lay motionless, bathed in clammy sweat; his eyes and mouth wide open; and the indecision of exhaustion cast a softened light on all his fancies—mere delirious dreams, which could never bear the faintset resemblance to reality.

Things must go on as they might, he lazily

Fate

thought; the future was still remote; he would think no more about it; he would let himself go with the chain of events, link by link; it was madness to double his fists against Fate, which was so strong—so omnipotent.

Fate

CHAPTER X

THE following days passed quietly enough, though a vague fear still hung over Bertie's head. He bowed that head without further thought, but still with a dull ferment in the depths of his heart, below the superficial calm.

Then one day he went with Frank to the Rhodeses, and Eva, taking his hand, said:

"We shall be good friends, shall we not?"

And after she had spoken he heard her voice still ringing in his ears like little bells. He mechanically let his velvety eyes rest on hers, and smiled, and allowed her to lead him to a sofa, and show him designs for furniture and patterns of curtains for their new home—her home and Frank's. Frank himself sat a little way off, talking to Sir Archibald. He looked at them, sitting side by side, like brother and sister, on the softly cushioned settee—their heads bent together over the rustling pages of the pattern-book, their hands meeting from time to time. And his brows were knit in a frown of displeasure.

And yet he laughed, and said to Eva:

Fate

"Bertie will be of the greatest use; he has far better taste than I."

And he felt as though he had spoken the words in spite of himself, or had meant to say something quite other than this compliment, but could not help it. All the time he was talking politics to Sir Archibald his eyes rested on them, magnetically attracted by their familiar manner.

There was a sisterly gentleness in Eva, an emanation of sympathy for her lover's friend, a somewhat romantic interest in the mystery of Van Maeren's fine dark eyes and insinuating voice, and a compassion for the deep Byronic sorrows which she attributed to him—something like the esthetic pathos of a sentimental reader over the inexplicable woes of a hero of romance.

It was to her a poetic friendship, which very harmoniously supplemented her love for Frank Westhove; a kind of love of which in her girlish enthusiasm she had never imagined the existence, and of which, if she could have suspected it, she would certainly never have thought herself capable: a calm, peaceful, and true affection, practical, almost homely, without the faintest tinge of romance; a love, not blind to her lover's faults, but faithful to him in spite of them, like a mother's for her undeserving child. She perceived his indolence over every voluntary effort, his indecision over every serious question, his vacil-

Fate

lation between this and that; and did not blind herself to all this weakness. But it was this very weakness which had gained her heart, as a pleasing contrast with the cool, uneffusive, sober affection of her father, who spoiled her indeed, but never so much as she herself desired.

Then there was another contrast which charmed her even more, which had filled her heart with an admiration that had become a passion; the contrast in Frank himself, of his mild, yielding character with the robust vigor of his stalwart person. She, woman as she was, found something adorable in the fact of this splendidly strong youth, with his broad chest and shoulders, his great mane of fair hair and powerful neck—this man, whose suppleness and ease in lifting and moving things betrayed constant practise in the use of his limbs—being so feeble in determination, and so gentle in demeanor. When she was alone and thought of him so, she could not help smiling, though the tears came into her eyes—tears of happiness—for this contrast made her happy. It was very strange, she thought, and she could not understand it; it was a riddle; but she did not try to solve it, for it was a riddle that she loved, and as she thought of it, with smiling lips and tear-dimmed eyes, she longed only to have her arms round his neck—her own Frank's.

She did not idealize him; she never now

Fate

thought of platonic twin-souls in superhuman
ecstasy; she took him as he was, a mere man; and
it was for what he was that she worshiped him,
calm and at rest in her worship. Although she
knew that the romantic side of her nature could
never find fulfilment—such as it now did through
her sisterly regard for Bertie—she had no regret
for it in her abounding love for Frank. And since
her nature found completion in the enjoyment of
the moment, she was pleased and quite satisfied,
and felt such a sunny glow in her and about her
as deserves to be called true happiness.

This was her frame of mind now, as she
looked through the patterns with Bertie, while
Frank sat chatting with her father. There was
the man she loved, here her brother-friend. This
was all good; she never could wish for anything
more than to be thus happy in her love and her
friendship. She looked at Bertie with a protecting and pitying smile, and yet with a touch of
contempt at his slight, boyish figure, his white
hands and diamond ring, his little feet in patent
leather shoes, hardly larger than her own; what
a dapper little mannikin he was. Always spot-
lessly precise in dress and manner, with an appealing cloud of melancholy over his whole person.

As he glanced up at her, consulting her about
some detail in one of the prints, Bertie detected
this smile on Eva's face, ironically patronizing

Fate

and at the same time kind and sisterly; and knowing that she liked him, he could to some extent read its meaning; but he asked her:

"What are you smiling at?"

"At nothing," said she; and she went on, still smiling affectionately: "Why did you never become an artist, Bertie?"

"An artist?" said Van Maeren, "what next?"

"A painter, or an author. You have great artistic taste—"

"I!" he repeated, much surprised, for he really did not know that he possessed very remarkable esthetic feeling, an exquisiteness of taste worthy of a woman, of a connoisseur; and her words set his own character before him in a new light. Does a man never know himself and what really lies in him?

"I could do nothing," he replied, somewhat flattered by Eva's speech; and in his astonishment, candid for once in spite of himself, he went on: "I should be too lazy."

He was startled by his own words, as though he had stripped himself bare; and he instinctively looked across at Frank to see if he had heard him. Vexed at his own thoughtlessness, he colored and laughed to hide his annoyance, while she, still smiling, shook her head reproachfully.

Fate

CHAPTER XI

WHEN, a little later, Eva was alone with her lover, and she showed him the patterns which his friend had preferred, Frank began: "Eva—"

She looked at him inquiringly, beaming with quiet happiness.

There was a turmoil in his brain: he wanted to speak to her about Bertie. But he suddenly remembered his promise to his friend never to reveal anything of his past life. Frank was a man who simply regarded a spoken word as inviolable, and he suddenly perceived that he could not say what he had on his tongue. And yet, he remembered his uncomfortable sensations when, on the top of Moldehoï, Eva had so innocently expressed her change of opinion in his friend's favor. Had he not then felt as though the black clouds were an omen of evil hanging over her head? And had he not experienced the same shudder as he saw them sitting side by side on the sofa, as if a noose were ready to cast round her neck? It was an instinctive dread, springing up unexpectedly, without anything to lead up to it.

Fate

Ought he not to speak, to tell her what Bertie was?
But he had promised—and it was foolishly super-
stitious to allow such an unreasoning terror to have
any influence on his mind. Bertie was not like
ordinary men; he was very lazy, and lived too con-
tentedly at the expense of others—a thing that
Westhove could not understand, and over which
in his good nature he simply shook his head with
a smile—but Bertie was not wicked. So he was
concealing nothing from Eva but that Bertie had
no money. Still, he had meant to say something;
something was seething in his brain. Eva was
looking at him wide-eyed; he must speak. So he
went on, embarrassed in spite of himself, coerced
by a mysterious force which seemed to dictate the
words:

"I was going to say—perhaps you will think me
silly—but I do not like, I do not think it right—"

She still looked at him with her surprised eyes,
smiling at his hesitancy. It was this very indecision which, in her eyes, was so engaging a contrast to his stalwart frame; she sat down on his
knee, leaning against him, and her voice sounded
like a poem of love:

"Well, what, Frank? My dearest Frank, what
is it?"

Her eyes smiled in his; she laid her arms round
his neck, clasping her hands, and again she asked:

"Tell me, foolish boy, what is the matter?"

Fate

"I do not like to see you always—that you should always—sit so—with Bertie."

The words forced their way against his will; and now that they were spoken it seemed to him that he had meant to say something quite different. Eva was amazed.

"Sit so with Bertie!" she repeated. "How do I sit with Bertie? Have I done anything I ought not? Or—tell me, Frank, are you so horribly jealous?"

He clasped her closer, and, kissing her hair, he muttered: "Yes, yes! I am jealous."

"But of Bertie—your best friend, who lives with you? You can not surely be jealous of him!"

She burst out laughing, and, carried away by her own mirth, fairly shook as she sat there, on his knee, with her head against his shoulder.

"Of Bertie!" she said, still gasping. "How is it possible? Oh, oh, of Bertie! But I only think of him as a pretty boy, almost a girl. He is so tiny, and has such neat little hands. Oh, oh! What! jealous of Bertie?"

"Do not laugh so!" he said, with a frown. "I really mean it—you are so familiar with him—"

"But he is your dearest friend!"

"Yes, so he may be—but yet—"

She began again to laugh; she thought him most amusing; and at the same time she loved him all the better for being so sullen and jealous.

Fate

"Silly fellow!" she said, and her fingers played with his fair, golden-tinted mustache. "How foolish—oh! how foolish you are!"

"But promise me—" he began again.

"Of course, if it will make your mind easy, I shall keep more at a distance. But I shall find it very difficult, for I am so accustomed to Bertie. And Bertie must not be allowed to guess it; thus your friendship will remain unbroken. I must still be good friends with him. No, no! I tell you I must be kind to him. Foolish boy that you are! I never knew that you could be so silly!" And she laughed again very heartily, shaking his head in her engaging merriment, and tousling his thick hair with her two little hands.

Fate

CHAPTER XII

FRANK had of late begun to think of Bertie as an intolerable burden. Though he himself did not understand why, he could not bear to see Eva and his friend together, and their intimacy brought this about almost every day. Eva had rightly perceived that she could hardly behave to Bertie otherwise than she had done hitherto. Meanwhile he had to put up with great coolness from Frank. After one of his escapades, which had lasted three days, this coolness was very conspicuous. Westhove, who usually made very pressing inquiries on his return from these mysterious absences, on this occasion said not a word. And Bertie vowed to himself that this should be the last of these disappearances.

But then came the discussion, which Van Maeren had so greatly dreaded; in a confidential moment his friend spoke of his impending marriage, and asked Bertie what plans he had for the future.

"For you know, dear old fellow," was Frank's kind way of putting it, "that I will with pleasure do my best to help you. Here, or in Holland, I

Fate

have a few connections. And so long as you have
nothing, of course I shall not leave you out in the
cold; on that you may safely reckon. But I shall
be leaving White-Rose Cottage: Eva thinks it too
much out of the way, and, as you know, prefers
Kensington. But we have had good times together, haven't we?"

And he clapped Bertie on the shoulder, grateful
for the life of good-fellowship they had enjoyed
within those walls, and feeling a little compassion
for the poor youth who took so kindly to the good
gifts of wealth, and who had, alas! no wealth to
procure them with. However, he penetrated no
further into Bertie's state of mind; he had always
had a turn for a Bohemian existence: he had known
luxury after living in misery; now life must be
a little less easy for him again. That was all.

Bertie, on his part, horrified by the heartless
villainy of his first reflections, allowed himself to
slide on day by day, with no further thought of
his various plots. He sometimes even had a naive
belief that at the last moment fortune would look
on him with favor: his Fatalism was like a form
of worship, giving him strength and hope.

However, a moment came when he thought all
hope lost; the danger was pressing and imminent.

"Bertie," said Westhove, who had just come
home in some excitement, "to-morrow you can
find some employment to suit you, I think. Tayle

Fate

—you know, our friend at the club—tells me that he wants to find a secretary for his father, Lord Tayle. The old man lives on his place, up in Northumberland; he is always ailing, and sometimes tiresome, still, it seems to me that you will not easily get such another chance. You will have a salary of eighty pounds, and live in the house of course. I should have spoken of you to Tayle at once, but that you begged me long ago—"

"Then you did not mention my name?" said Bertie, hastily and almost offended.

"No," replied Frank, surprised at his tone. "I could make no overtures till I had spoken to you. But make up your mind at once, for Tayle has two other men in his eye already. If you can decide at once I will go back to Tayle this minute: my cab is waiting." And he took up his hat.

Eighty pounds, and a position as secretary, with free quarters at the Castle! How the splendor of such an offer would have dazzled Bertie not so very long since, in America. But now—

"My dear Frank," he said, very coldly, "I am very much obliged for your kind intentions, but, pray, take no trouble on my account. I can not accept the place. Dismiss your cab—"

"What!" cried his friend, in utter amazement. "Will you not at least think it over?"

"Thank you very much. If you have nothing better to offer me than to become the servant of the father of a man with whom I have been intimate as an equal, I can only say, Thank you for nothing. I am not going to shut myself up in a country-house, and scribble for an ailing, fractious old man, for a pittance of eighty pounds a year. And what would Tayle think of me? He has always known me as your friend, and we have been familiar on that footing; and now he is to see me his father's hired menial! I can not say that you have much delicate feeling, Frank."

His brain was in a whirl while he spoke; never before had he assumed such a haughty tone in addressing Frank, but it was like a cry of despair rising up from the ruins of his false pride.

"But, good God, man! what do you expect?" exclaimed Westhove. "You know all my friends, and it is only through my friends that I can hope to help you."

"I will take no help from any one like the men of our own club, nor from any one to whom you have introduced me as their equal."

"That certainly makes the case a difficult one," said Westhove, with a sharp laugh, for great wrath was rising up in him. "Then you have nothing to say to this?"

"Nothing."

"But what on earth do you want?" said Frank, indignantly.

"For the moment, nothing."

"For the moment—well and good; but by and by?"

"That I will see all in good time. And if you can not be more considerate—"

He stopped short, startled by his own voice. He was speaking loudly—as it would seem with domineering vehemence, but in fact only with the energy of despairing indolence and pride at bay. The two men looked at each other for a few seconds, each suddenly feeling as though he had a store of buried grievances against the other—grievances which had accumulated in spite of the friendly intimacy of their lives, and which they were on the point now of flinging in each other's teeth as foul insults.

But Van Maeren checked his outburst. He recollected himself, or he had not forgotten himself. He smiled and held out his hand:

"Forgive me, Frank," he said, humbly, with that voice like beaten gold, and that mitigating smile; "I know you meant well. I can never, no, never, repay you for all you have done for me. But this place I can not really accept. I would rather be a waiter, or the conductor of a tram-car. Forgive me if I seem ungrateful."

So they made it up. But Westhove thought this pride on his companion's part ridiculous, and was vexed that the whole affair must remain a secret from Eva. He would have liked to consult her on the subject. And it was with a deeper frown and more scowling glance that he watched those two, Bertie and Eva, as they sat side by side in the evening in the subdued light of the blue-shaded lamp, chatting like brother and sister. It was like some covert dishonesty. It was all he could do to keep from proclaiming aloud that Bertie was a parasite, a low fellow, from tearing them apart, from snatching them away from their blissful smiling and guileless intimacy as they discussed furniture and hangings.

Fate

CHAPTER XIII

AFTER this ineffectual attempt to help Van Maeren his friend took no further trouble, expecting that when the case became urgent Bertie himself would ask his assistance. But Bertie's refusal led Frank to perceive for the first time the false position in which he had placed his companion, both with regard to himself and to his associates; his kindness to a friend out of luck in allowing him to live for a year as a man of fortune struck him now—seen in the light of an attachment which had purified, renovated, and transformed his whole nature—as indescribably preposterous, as trampling on every law of honor and veracity; an unjustifiable mockery of the good faith of the world he lived in. Formerly he had thought all this very amusing, but now he felt that it was mean, base, to have enjoyed such amusement as this. And he understood that he had himself encouraged the growth, as of some poisonous weed, of Van Maeren's false pride, which now forbade him to accept a favor from any one of their boon companions.

The days glided by, and Westhove could not

shake off the sense of self-reproach, which, indeed, grew upon him as time went on. Van Maeren cast a shadow over the happiness of his love. Eva saw that some dull grief made him silent; he would sit brooding for many minutes at a time— his brows knit and a deep furrow across his forehead.

"What ails you, Frank?"

"Nothing, my darling."

"Are you still jealous?"

"No. I will cure myself of it."

"Well, you see, it is your own fault; if you had not always sung the praises of Bertie as your best friend I should never have become so intimate with him."

Yes, it was his own fault; that he saw very clearly.

"And are you satisfied with me now?" she asked, laughing.

He, too, laughed. For indeed it was true; for Frank's sake she had now suddenly changed her behavior to Bertie; she would rise and quit the sofa where they sat while he was yet speaking; she sometimes contradicted him, reproached him for his foppishness, and laughed at him for his dainty little hands. He looked at her in amazement, fancied she meant it for flirtation, but could not understand what she would be at. One evening, for hour after hour she pestered him with petty annoyances, pin-pricks, which she intended should reassure Frank and not wound Bertie too deeply. The conversation presently turned on heraldry, and Sir Archibald wanted to show the two men the blazoned roll of his family tree. Frank rose, ready to follow him to his study, and Bertie did the same. Eva felt a little compunction, thinking she had carried her teasing rather far this time, and she knew that her father's pedigree would not interest him in the least.

"Leave Bertie here, papa," said she. "He knows nothing about heraldry."

And, at the same time, to comfort Frank, who dared not betray his jealousy, she added lightly, with a mollifying twinkle of her long eyelashes:

"Frank will trust us alone together, I dare say!"

Her voice was so simple, her glance so loving, that Frank smiled and nodded trustfully, though annoyed at seeing Bertie sit down again.

As soon as they were alone Bertie began:

"For shame, Eva, how could you torment me as you have been doing?"

She laughed and blushed, a little ashamed of herself for treating him so to please Frank. But Bertie's face was grave, and with an appealing gesture he folded his hands, and said beseechingly: "Promise me that you will not do so again."

Fate

She gazed at him in surprise at his earnest tone:

"It is only my fun," said she.

"But a form of fun which is suffering to me," he replied in a low voice.

And still she looked at him, not understanding. He sat huddled up, his head on his breast, his eyes fixed before him, and his brown hair, which waved a little over his forehead, clinging to his temples, which were damp with perspiration. He was evidently much agitated. He had no idea what might come of this dialogue, but he was aware that his tone had been solemn, that these first words might be the prelude to a very important interview. He felt that these few minutes were destined to become a precious link in the chain of his life, and he waited with the patience of a fatalist for the thoughts which should take shape in his brain, and the words which should rise to his lips. He kept an eye on himself, as it were, and at the same time spun a web about Eva, as a spider entangles a fly in the thread it draws out of its bowels.

"You see," he went on slowly, "I can not bear that you should torment me so. You think less well of me than you used. But if I have little hands, I can not help it."

She could not forbear a smile at the intentionally coquettish tone he had assumed, an affectation of spoiled-childishness which she saw through at once. But she replied, nevertheless:

"Well, I beg your pardon for teasing you. I will not do so again."

He, however, had risen from his chair, and, pretending not to see the hand she held out, he silently went to the window, and stood there, looking out on the park-like greenery of Kensington Gardens, dimmed with mist. She sat still, waiting for him to speak; but he said nothing.

"Are you angry, Bertie?"

Then he slowly turned round. The gray daylight fell through the muslin curtains, and gave a pallid look—a hue of Parian china—to his delicate features. Very gently, with a deep, melancholy smile, he shook his head in negation. And to her romantic fancy the sadness of that smile gave him a poetic interest as of a youthful god or a fallen angel; the celestial softness of a sexless mythological being, such as she had seen in illustrated books of verse; a man in form, a woman in face. She longed to invite him to pour out his woes; and at this moment it would scarcely have surprised her if his speech had sounded like a rhythmical monologue, a long lament in blank verse.

"Bertie, my dear fellow, what is the matter?"

There he stood speechless, in the pale slanting light, knowing that the effect must be almost theatrical. And she, sitting where it was darker, could see that his eyes glistened through tears. Much moved, she went up to him; she took his hand, and made him sit down by her side.

"Speak, Bertie, have I vexed you? Can you not tell me?"

But again he shook his head, with that faint smile. And at last he said huskily:

"No, Eva, I am not vexed. I can be vexed no more. But I am very, very sad because we must so soon part, and I care for you so much—"

"Part! Why? Where are you going?"

"Indeed, I do not myself know that, sweet girl. I shall remain till you are married, and then I must go, to wander hither and thither quite alone. Will you sometimes think of me, I wonder?"

"But why do you not stay in London?"

He looked at her. He had begun this conversation without knowing whither it might lead him, abandoning himself to chance. But now, with this look which her eyes met in response, there suddenly blazed up in him a little diabolical flame. He knew now what he was driving at; he weighed every word he uttered as if they were grains of gold; he felt himself very lucid, very logical and calm, free from the painful, incoherent agitation of the last few minutes. And he spoke very slowly, in a mournful, hollow voice like a sick man:

Fate

"In London! No, Eva, I can not remain here."

"Why not?"

"I can not, dear girl. I can not, not with any decency. It is impossible."

The hypocrisy of his eye, the languor of his tone, his assumption of inconsolable grief, distilled into her mind a vague suspicion like an insidious poison —the suspicion that it was on her account that he could not remain in London, because he would have to meet her as his friend's wife. It was no more than a suggestion. The wordless despair which seemed to exhale from him inspired the in-ference. But her mind rebelled against it; it was a mere suspicion and groundless. He went on, still very slowly, considering every word as if with mathematical accuracy. "And when I am gone and you are left with Frank, always with him, will you be happy, Eva?"

"Why, Bertie?" She paused. It would be almost cruel to say "Yes," in the security of her happiness, in the face of his pain.

"Why do you ask?" she said, almost timidly.

He gazed into her face with the deep, soft, misty blackness of his fine eyes. Then he bent his head, and they filled with tears, and he clutched his hands as if they were cold.

"Why—why?" Eva insisted.

"Nothing, nothing. Promise me that you will

be happy. For if you were not happy I should be heartbroken."

"What should hinder my being happy; I love Frank so dearly?" she exclaimed, though still fearing lest she should hurt his feelings.

"Yes; and so long as you are happy all is well," he murmured low, still rubbing his hands.

Then, on a sudden, while her inquiring gaze still rested on his face, he said: "Poor child!"

"What—why poor child?" she asked in dismay.

He seized her hands, his tears dropped on her fingers.

"Oh, Eva, Eva! God, who can read my heart— If you—oh! I feel such pity, such great, passionate pity for you. I would do I know not what—I would give my life if I—if you . . . Poor, poor child!"

She was standing up now, trembling, and as pale as death; her fingers clutched the table-cover, which slipped as she pulled it, and a glass vase, in which a few flowers were fading, was upset; the water trickled over the velvet cloth in great silvery beads. She let it flow into pools, staring at it with wide, terrified eyes, while he covered his face with his hands.

"Bertie," she cried, "oh, Bertie! Why do you speak thus? What is it all? Tell me. Tell me everything. I must know. I desire you to speak out."

Fate

His reply was a gesture—a perfectly natural gesture of deprecation, with no touch of theatrical insincerity, a gesture as though he would retract his words, and had said something he should have kept to himself; then he, too, rose, and his face had changed; its expression was no longer one of suffering or of pity, but of cool decision.

"No, no. There is nothing to tell, Eva."

"Nothing! And you could exclaim, 'Poor child!' And you pity me! Good God, but why? What is this—what evil threatens me?" She had Frank's name on her lips, but dared not utter it, and he was conscious of this.

"Nothing, really and truly, nothing, dear Eva. I assure you, nothing. I sometimes have the most foolish thoughts, mere fancies. Look, the vase has fallen over."

"But what were you thinking then—what fancies?"

He wiped the water off the table-cloth with his pocket handkerchief, and replaced the flowers in the glass.

"Nothing; nothing at all," he murmured, huskily; he was tremulous with nervousness, and his tone was deeply compassionate, as if his words were meant to shroud some awful secret. Then, as he said no more, she sank on the sofa and broke into uncontrolled and passionate sobs, scared by the undefinable terror which rose up in her soul.

Fate

"Eva, dear Eva, be calm!" he entreated her, fearing lest some one should come into the room. And then—then he knelt down close by her, taking her hands, and pressing them tenderly.

"Look at me, Eva. I assure you; I swear to you there is nothing wrong—nothing at all, but what exists in my own imagination. But, you see, I care for you so fondly: you will let me say so, won't you? For what I feel for you is only guileless, devoted friendship for my friend's bride and my own little sister. I love you so truly that I can not help asking myself, Will my dear Eva be happy? It is a foolish thought, no doubt; but in me it is not strange, because I am always thinking of those I love. You see, I have known so much sorrow and suffering. And when I see any one I care for so truly as I do for you—see her so full of confidence in life and of fair illusions, the thought comes over me, terrible, but irresistible: Will she be happy? Is there, indeed, any such thing as happiness? Oh, I ought not to say such things; I only darken your outlook, and give you pessimistic notions; but sometimes when I see you with Frank, my heart is so full! For I love Frank, too. I owe so much to him, and I should so gladly see him happy with some woman—with some one— Still, I can only say, trust wholly in Frank. He loves you, though he is a little fickle, a little capricious in his feelings; but he adores you. The delicate shades of a woman's nature are above his comprehension, perhaps, and he is apt to carry his light-heartedness a little too far—still, he means no harm. He is so candid, so honest; you know always so exactly what he is at. And so, Eva, dear Eva, never let any misunderstanding come between you—always be open with each other; will you not, my child. Oh, my poor Eva!"

And he, too, sobbed low in his mysterious anguish, which was not altogether a pretense, for he was really in despair at the prospect before him. She looked down on him in dismay, greatly distressed by his words, from which she inferred something which he would not reveal: each word a drop of subtle venom, and the germ of strange doubts, which shot up like poisonous weeds.

"Then there is nothing to tell?" she said once more, in a weary tone of entreaty, clasping her hands.

"No, dear Eva, nothing at all. Only I am worn out, you see—quite an old man—and so I worry myself sometimes about you two. When I am far away—far from London—will you be happy? Tell me, Eva, will you be happy? Promise me, swear to me that you will."

She gently nodded in the affirmative, with a sigh of regret that he must leave London—regret for what he had suggested, worst of all for what he had left unsaid: the mystery, the terror! He, meanwhile, had risen; holding out his hands to her, and shaking his head, as though over the follies of man, he said, with his most pathetic smile:

"How silly you must think me, to torment myself so about nothing. I ought not to have said so much; perhaps I have saddened you with it all. Have I?"

"No," she replied with a gentle smile, shaking her head. "No, not really."

He let himself drop into a chair, sighing deeply.

"Alas! such is life!" he murmured, with a fixed gaze full of sinister significance. She made no answer, her heart was too full.

By this time it was dark. Van Maeren took his leave. Frank alone had been asked to stay to dinner.

"Have you forgiven me?" he asked, very humbly, with his most insinuating and romantic air, as the last rays of daylight shed an ethereal glow on his face.

"For what?" she said, but she was silently weeping.

"For having distressed you, even for a minute?"

She nodded, and rose, trembling, exhausted, and tottering.

"Oh, yes; you gave me a great fright. But you will not do so again, I beg."

"Never," he murmured.

He kissed her hand; a courteous caress he was

accustomed to bestow, with a touch of foppery like an eighteenth century marquis; and he went away.

She was left alone. Standing there, in the middle of the room, she closed her eyes, and she felt as though a mist had fallen and enwrapped her. And in that mist she saw Moldehoï and the spectral fjord gleaming between the two ranges of protecting mountains, and far away, in the west, those three thin bars of gold. And suddenly she felt, as she had never felt before, so forlorn, so lonely, in the midst of the cloud, without even a thought of Sir Archibald and Frank, remembering nothing but her long dead mother. A weight pressed on her brain, like the icy palm of a giant's hand; dusky gloom closed in upon her, and suddenly the living warmth within her was chilled as with a deadly frost. She felt as if she were standing in vast space, and through it—invisible, intangible, and yet sensibly and undeniably real—she was aware of a coming horror, rolling dully on like distant thunder. She stretched out her hands, feeling for some support. But she did not fall senseless; she recovered herself; and found that she was still in the middle of the room, now almost dark, a little tremulous, and with a feeble sensation about the knees. And she could not but think that there was something yet—something which Bertie had concealed from her.

Fate

CHAPTER XIV

NEXT day she thought it all over once more. What was it? What was it? Would Bertie have pitied her so if there really had been nothing in it but his own pessimistic fears for her happiness? Or was he not indeed hiding something? And had it anything to do with Frank?

And then Frank came, and she often saw him sit quite still for a time, with a frown on his brow.

"What is the matter?" she asked. And he replied just as usual:

"Nothing, sweetheart."

And they chatted together, at first a little constrained, but soon quite happy again in their plans and dreams, forgetting what weighed on their minds. Eva would laugh brightly, and perch herself on Frank's knee, and play with his mustache. But if Bertie came in, something seemed at once to come between them; a shadow which parted them.

It was when the friends were alone together that they were most ill at ease. Then Westhove could only long to turn Van Maeren out of doors at once, without the smallest perceptible cause, like a

Fate

mangy hound. He pictured Bertie as he had seen him standing shivering in his wretched raiment that snowy night. Now he was such a dandy, and nothing was too good for him; and he was irreproachable; he did not even go off for a few days at a time, wandering obscurely like a cat. He was always "interesting," with his halo of melancholy; and since the scene over the secretaryship, he often assumed a reproachful tone in his voice and expression when speaking to Frank.

Eva, when left to herself, was deeply wretched. Chaotic doubts tortured her soul, doubts which, for the moment, she could set aside, but which would force themselves on her as soon as she thought of Bertie's sympathetic smile and strange compassion for her. Oh! what was it? What was it? She had often meant to talk it over with Frank, but when she was on the point of beginning the subject, she did not know what to say. That Bertie pitied her? It could be nothing but his own pessimism which, in its universal humanity, regarded the world as worthy of pity, since it seemed created to be wretched.

Should she ask Frank whether he had any silent grief—if he had anything to trouble him? This she did once or twice, and the answer was always the same:

"Nothing, dearest!"

What then, oh, what was this horror? Alas!

she could get no further; she stood as it were blind-fold in an enchanted circle, which she could not overstep, and her hand felt all round, but could grasp nothing. If she resolutely banished such thoughts they came back again persistently. They overwhelmed her afresh, they repossessed themselves of her brain, suggesting endless doubts; and ending always, always, in the same question which was the invariable outcome of these miserable cogitations:

"What can it be? Is there anything at all?"

And never an answer.

She had once again questioned Bertie; but he had only smiled, with that terrifying smile of woe, and had implored her not to rack her brain over anything which he might have inconsiderately let drop as the natural outcome of his melancholy temper. Otherwise, he should henceforth always be afraid of speaking to her with any frankness; he must weigh his words, and their confidential intimacy as brother and sister would be at an end. And her own feeling in the matter was full of dubious half-lights, in which no outline was distinct, no color decided—a confusion of shadowy gray tints which dimmed the clear brightness of her love with increasing gloom, fatiguing her spirit by their indefiniteness, their non-existence in actual life, and their intangible semblance of reality, like a dream.

Fate

Once, however, the dream took substance; once she touched—she saw—she heard—something. But was that it?

They were coming out of the Lyceum. The crowd streamed forth, slowly shuffling, pushing impatiently now and then, shoulder to shoulder. And in the crush, close to her, Eva saw the flaming red plush opera-cloak of a tall, stout woman, and under a babyish "cherry-ripe" hat a face, rose, white and black, with a doll-like smile, which suddenly leaned across her to address Frank. The brim of the hat rested on a mass of yellow curls, a scent of musk and rice-powder greeted her nostrils, and, like a blow in her own face, she heard the words:

"Hallo! good-evening, Frank; how are you, old boy?"

She started and shrank back, looking hastily first at the rouged face and then at Frank; she saw his flashing look of rage, nor did the tall woman's confusion escape her notice—a damsel of the skating-rink—though the stranger drew back at seeing a lady on Frank's arm; she had evidently at first seen him over Eva's head in the crowd, and she now vanished, disconcerted by her own blunder in addressing a man who had a lady with him.

But she shot a glance of amazed inquiry at Van Maeren who was close behind. Bertie might have warned her; for it was Bertie who had whispered

Fate

three words under the "cherry-ripe" hat, with a nod toward the front, saying: "There goes Frank."

She was vexed with herself; but she really had not seen the young lady.

When they reached home, Sir Archibald, who had observed nothing, was bidding them goodnight at the door, but Frank exclaimed: "I beg your pardon—but I must speak to Eva—I beg of you—"

It was already late, but Sir Archibald was no stickler for etiquette.

They were alone, looking at each other with anxious eyes, but neither spoke. Frank began hurriedly, stumbling over his words as if he were eager to forestall any evil suspicion she might entertain.

"Eva, believe me, Eva; you must believe me; it was nothing. You must not think anything of —of what happened just now."

In a few brief words he told of a former acquaintance—a young man's acquaintance—of the skating-rink. This was all at an end, it was a thing of the past; she must know that every man had a past. She knew that—surely?

"A past," she echoed coldly. "Oh! every man has a past? But we—we have no past."

"Eva, Eva!" he cried, for through the irony of her tone there pierced such acute pain that he stood dismayed and helpless, not knowing how to comfort her.

"Tell me only this much," she went on, going close up to him and looking into his face with that strange stare. She laid her hands on his shoulders and tried to read his inmost soul through his eyes. And she slowly said, expecting to hear her own doom in the first word he should utter:

"It is at an end?"

He fell on his knees before her where she had dropped on a chair, rigidly upright, as if she were frozen; he warmed her resisting hands in his grasp —and he swore that it was. His oath rang true; truth was stamped on his face; and she believed him. He besought forgiveness, told her that she must never think of it again, that all men—

"Oh, yes," she nodded her comprehension. "I know, I understand. Papa has brought me up on rather liberal lines."

He recollected that phrase; she had used it once before. And they both at once remembered Moldehoï and the black clouds. Eva shuddered.

"Are you cold, dearest?"

But she shook her head, still with a strange light in her eyes. He would have clasped her in his arms, but she drew back, and he felt himself rebuffed, almost rejected. He could not understand her. Why no kiss, why no generous reconciliation, if she understood so well, if she had been so liberally trained? But she was perhaps a little upset; he would not be too urgent. It would no doubt blow over.

When he was gone, Eva, in her own room, shivered and her teeth chattered as if she had an ague. And she began to cry bitterly, miserably, with deep despairing sobs, for grief that she lived, that she was a rational being—a woman—above all, that she had ever loved; that the world existed, that everything was so mean, so base—a mud-heap! She loathed it all. She felt as if she had never really understood any of the books she had read; neither the "Faery Queen" nor "Ghosts"—especially "Ghosts"; never understood anything she had learned under her father's "rather liberal" training. The white-feathery down of her illusions was blown into space; a rough hand had rubbed away the bloom from her most secret and inmost soul; the sacred innocence of her maidenhood had been dragged in the gutter. For the first time the peace of her great but reasonable love for Frank came into violent collision with the romance of her girlish dreams, and the balance of the two feelings was destroyed—of the practical and the romantic side of her character.

Fate

But that talk with Eva had been the first step on a downward path, where it was now impossible to turn back. A singular lucidity of thought dawned in his brain, as though his brain were a crystal mirror, in which his ideas were reflected in a vivid light. Never yet had he felt himself so keenly alert, so clearly logical; never had he aimed so true at an object in view, with the precision of a needle. The clearness of his mind was so perfect that in a naive perception of his own baseness— a lucid moment of self-knowledge which once flashed on him, to his surprise, for no more than a second—he wondered that he should not apply so much talent and ingenuity to a nobler purpose.

"Why did you never become an artist?" he could hear Eva asking him.

But he only smiled; the practical weariness of life rose up before him; his own indolence, his catlike love of physical ease. No, no, he could not help himself; so it must be. The first step was taken. It was Fate!

Then, that evening as they came out of the theatre, that woman who belonged to their past life, his own significant nod, and his words, "There goes Frank." Was not all this, too, a fatality? Did not Fate strew such trivial incidents as these in the path of those who burned incense at her shrine and paid her due worship, to be utilized by them as benefits—infinitely small

Fate

CHAPTER XV

AFTER that conversation with Eva, Bertie felt as though he were living in a more subtle atmosphere, wandering in a labyrinth full of mysterious ways of craft and cunning, in which he must walk very circumspectly if he did not wish to lose himself. He knew very well what he had been driving at; he wanted to instil into Eva suspicions of Frank's constancy. Did she not herself know her lover to be fickle, almost capricious? Had not his hints been well chosen? Had he not sown the seed of doubt? He did not know. He saw nothing to reassure him in the regular, monotonous routine of everyday life, in which subtle shades of manner so often escape even the keenest observer. Eva had, indeed, once asked him about that Something; but after that, in appearance at least, their intercourse had been on the old footing again. He saw no difference in Eva—none in Frank; so Eva could have said nothing to her lover and asked him no questions.

Before that afternoon Bertie had known hesitancy, had felt some disgust at his own heartlessness, some horror of his own monstrous selfishness.

Fate

links, which they must themselves weld into the chain? Did not Fate give men the illusion of free will, and a semblance of truth to the lie which says that they by their own energy can coerce the course of circumstance? No more than a word, a nod—"There goes Frank!"—and then, for the rest, trust to the chance— Chance! What is chance?—that the smart damsel of the skating-rink should overlook Eva—tiny, dainty Eva—lost in the crowd.

Had the result been such as he had counted on? Had he guessed the purpose of Fate? Yes, he thought, in some small degree; why else should Frank have craved an interview with Eva at so late an hour And so, in that atmosphere of finely spun cunning, in that labyrinth of wiles, he no longer regarded himself as base, heartless, selfish. Words—mere words! It was folly to consider things too closely; he dismissed all scruples, and if they would sometimes force themselves on him he would argue with himself: Who could tell whether it was not a good thing if Frank should not marry? He was not a man to marry—no, really; he was changeable, capricious, and inconstant; he would not make a wife happy.

Still, Van Maeren could see at once that this was self-deception; and he would laugh to himself, shaking his head, at finding himself so droll, so singular. Life was as nothing; nothing was worth troubling one s self about; but this introspection, this self-study, looking into one's own mind, juggling with one's own thoughts—that was really interesting, that was an amusing occupation, while lying at full length on a comfortable sofa.

And yet he seldom enjoyed any repose of mind. The web of his scheming was perpetually being wearily woven in his mind. His interviews with Eva were a fatiguing effort—sometimes a long discourse, sometimes only half utterances—for he had constantly and precisely to weigh every word. Still, this weariness was never to be detected in his air and manner, or in the phrases which fell from his lips, so apparently unpremeditated that they seemed alive with natural impulse. They were, in fact, the outcome of theatrical and carefully elaborated pessimism; they were lamentations over the ills of life, pity for Eva, wrapped in mysterious regrets; and amid all this melancholy, accusations against Westhove—mere trifles, passing hints, amounting to nothing but for the tone and accent—accusations of levity, inconstancy, caprice, fickleness. But at the slightest outry on Eva's part he was ready to contradict himself, fencing cleverly enough, now with himself, and now with Eva, with all the feints of a master of the foils, just touching her lightly—a prick here and a prick there—drawing a tiny drop of blood at each hit.

And to Eva it seemed that her soul, after having

been dragged through a gutter, was bleeding to death under these pin-pricks. It was a very sensible pain when she hopelessly compared the reality with her dreams, as they grew more vague and faded away, when she argued with herself in the cold light of reason, and asked herself, "Why am I so wretched? Because Frank is a young man like other young men; because Bertie is a pessimist, and despairs of my ever being happy?" And then she would shrug her shoulders; her trouble was intangible, had paled to a thin cloud, and vanished. She had always been very happy; Bertie's dejection was sickly nonsense; she should be happy again. But, notwithstanding that her common sense thus dissipated the pain, it constantly returned in spite of reason and argument; returned persistently, like an object tossed on a wave, which comes and goes, comes and goes.

She could endure it no longer, and one day when she ventured to look honestly into her own heart, she saw that she did indeed doubt Frank, and the truth of his statements about that woman. Longing for some certainty, she asked Bertie—his friend:

"Tell me, Bertie—that Something of which you once spoke to me; that mystery: what is it?"

"Oh, nothing, my dear girl, absolutely nothing."

She gazed at him with penetrating eyes, and went on in a strange, cold tone:

Fate

"Well; but I know; I have guessed."

Bertie was startled. What was she thinking? what had she got into her head?"

"Yes, I have guessed it," she repeated. "Frank does not love me; he loves—he loves that woman —that creature of the Lyceum. He has always loved her; is it so?"

Bertie said nothing, but stared before him; that was the easiest and best reply.

"Bertie, tell me, is it so?"

"No, it is not so," he answered, dully. "What a foolish notion to have got into your head. What made you think of such a thing?" But there was no ring of conviction in his voice; he spoke mechanically, as though in absence of mind, as if he were thinking of something else.

"Does he ever see her now?" she went on, feeling as if she were defiling herself with her own words; as if her lips were dropping slime.

"Why, of course not. What are you thinking of?"

She leaned back with a sigh, and tears glistened in her large eyes. He was silent for a minute, studying her out of the corner of his eye. Then, as if to mitigate his too feeble repudiation of the suspicion, he went on reproachfully:

"Really, Eva, you must not think such things of Frank. It is not nice; you must have some confidence in the man you are to marry."

Fate

"Then it is not the truth?"

"Certainly not. He never sees her now."

"But does not he think of her still?"

He gave her a long, deep, enigmatical look. His eyes were like black velvet darkness; she could not read their meaning.

"Fie!" said he, reprovingly, and he shook his head.

"That is no answer," she said, urgently. And again he fixed that dark gaze on her.

"Good God! answer me!" she cried, her heart wrung to the very core.

"How can you expect me to know Frank's feelings?" he dared to murmur. "I don't know— there!"

"Then it is so?" she moaned, clutching his hands.

"I don't know," he repeated, and, freeing himself from her grasp, he turned away and rose.

"He loves her; he can not live without her; he is that creature's slave, as you men sometimes are to such women; and though he sees her no more, out of respect for me, he thinks of her and talks of her to you—and that is why he is so silent and grave when he is here: Is it so?"

"Good Heavens! I do not know," he groaned, with mild impatience. "How should I know?"

"But why then does he pretend to love me? Why did he ask me to marry him? Because once, for a moment in Norway, he fancied he could do without her? Because he meant to live a new life, and now finds that he can not?" She clasped her hands with a gesture of anguish.

"Good God, Eva! say no more—say no more. I do not know, I tell you—I know nothing about it—nothing."

He sank back in his chair with a sigh of exhaustion. She said no more; the tears streamed from her eyes like rain impossible to be restrained.

Fate

CHAPTER XVI

AND in her misery she thought she had been very clever and cunning, and that she had guessed rightly; while, in truth, as guileless as a child, she had been as it were hypnotized by his magnetic gaze, and had spoken the very words he had intended she should utter.

She felt nothing of this; she saw him still as her brother-friend, fragile, affectionate, and unhappy, dreading to wound her, anxious to screen her from the truth for fear of hurting her, and yet not crafty enough to conceal it when she pressed him too closely. This was how he appeared to her. Not for an instant did she suspect that she was as a fly wrapping itself closer and closer in the spider's toils.

Bertie himself, after this scene, failed to see clearly that he had pulled the wires; that he had been the first to taint her confidence with the poison of suspicion; that he had brought about the catastrophe as they came out of the Lyceum; that he had compelled Eva to follow the clue he had chosen to suggest. Dimness shrouded the clearness of his mental vision, as a breath clouds

Fate

a mirror; the lucid crisis of his faculties was past.
This was all the outcome of circumstances, he
thought; no human being of his own free will
could work such things out— How easily everything had come about, how simply, without a
hitch! It was because Fate had so willed it and
had favored him—he had no part in it. Nor was
this self-deception: he really thought so.

In the evening after their last interview, Eva
went, very late, to seek her father in his study,
where he sat reading his books on heraldry. He
supposed she had come to bid him good-night, as
usual; but she sat down facing him, very upright,
and with a set face like a sleep-walker.

"Father, I want to speak to you."

He looked at her in surprise. In the Olympian
peace of his genealogical studies, in the calm,
emotionless existence of a hale old man, who finds
a solace for advancing years among his books, he
had never discerned that a drama was going on
close beside him, played by three beings whom he
saw every day. And he was startled at his daughter's rigid face and tone of suppressed suffering.

"Are you ill, my child?"

"Oh, no, I am quite well. But I want to ask you
something. I want to know if you will speak to
Frank?"

"To Frank?"

"Yes. To Frank. The other evening as we were

coming out of the Lyceum—" And she told him the whole story, sitting straight up in her chair, with that strange look in her face, and a husky, subdued voice; all about the yellow-haired woman, and her own suspicions and distrust. It was wrong of her to doubt Frank, but really she could not help it. She would fain have quoted Bertie as evidence, but Bertie had after all said nothing definite, so she did not see how she could bring him into court, and did not therefore mention his name.

Sir Archibald listened in dismay. He had never suspected what was going on in his daughter's mind; he had always supposed that everything was as clear as the sun at noon.

"And—what then?" he asked in some embarrassment.

"And then—I want you to speak to Frank. Ask him pointblank whether he still loves this woman, who has played some part in his past life; whether he can not bear to give her up; whether that is the reason he is always so silent and gloomy when we see him here. Get him to speak out. I would rather hear my doom than live in this dreadful suspense. And to you, perhaps, he will clear it all up, so that things may go on as they were before. Say nothing of my distrust; if it is not justified by the facts it might make him angry. It is too bad of me to suspect his truth, and I have tried to bring myself to a better mind; but I can not succeed. There is something in it, I know not what. There is something in the air about me—oh! what, I know not—which whispers to me: 'Do not trust him, do not trust him.' I can not understand what it is, but I feel it in me, all about me! It is a voice in my ear; sometimes an eye which gazes at me. At night, when I can not sleep, it looks down on me; it speaks to me; I feel as if I were going crazy. Perhaps it is a spirit! But do you speak to him, papa. Do that much for your child. I am so very, very unhappy."

She knelt at his feet and laid her head on his knees, sobbing bitterly. He mechanically stroked her hair, but he did not in the least understand. He loved his child, but his affection was more a matter of tender habit than of sympathetic intelligence. He did not understand her; he thought her foolish and fanciful. Was it for this that he had given her a first-rate education, let her read all kinds of books, and made her know the world as it was—stern, practical, and selfish, a struggle in which each one must endeavor to conquer and secure a place and a share of happiness, by sheer calm determination? He had his own corner in it, with his books and his heraldry; why did she let herself be a victim to nervous fancies? For it was all nerves—nothing but nerves! Cursed things were nerves! How like her mother she was, in

Fate

spite of her liberal education! Dreamy, romantic, full of absurd imagination. He speak to Frank? Why—what about—what was he to say? The lady at the Lyceum; this woman or that, to whom he had bowed? That might happen to any one. Eva was very absurd not to see that it might. And as to his talking it over with Frank—why, the young man would think that his future father-in-law was a perfect fool. There were thousands of such women in London. Where was the young man who had no acquaintance among them? And the picture of disturbed peace, of an unpleasant discussion, which would destroy an hour or perhaps a day of his Olympian repose and tear him from his studies, rose up in his brain, a terror to his simple-minded selfishness.

"Come, Eva, this is sheer folly," he good-humoredly grumbled. "What good do you think I can do? These are mere sickly fancies."

"No, no. They are not sickly fancies; not fancies at all. It is something—something quite different. There is something in me, around me—beyond my control."

"But, child, you are talking nonsense!"

"When I try to think it out, it goes away for a little while; but then it comes back again."

"Really, Eva, you must not talk so foolishly. After all, what is this story you have told me; what does it all mean? It comes and it goes, and it stays away, and then again it comes and goes."

She shook her head sadly, sitting on the floor at his feet in front of the fire.

"No, no," she said, very positively. "You do not understand, you are a man; you do not understand all there is in a woman. We women are quite different. But you will speak to him, will you not, and ask him all about it?"

"No, Eva; that I certainly will not. Frank might very well ask me what business it was of mine. You know as well as I do that every man has, or has had, acquaintance among such women. There is nothing in that. And Frank strikes me as too honorable to have anything to do with one of them now that he is engaged to you. I know him too well to imagine that. It is really too silly of you—do you hear: too silly!"

She began to sob passionately, and moan in an overpowering fit of grief. She wrung her hands, rocking herself from side to side, as if suffering intolerable torments.

"Oh, papa!" she entreated. "Dear papa, do, do! Do this for your child's sake, your little Eva. Go to him, talk to him. I am so unhappy, I can not bear it, I am so wretched! Speak to him; I can not speak of such a matter. I am only a girl, and it is all so horrible, so sickening. Oh, papa, papa, do speak to Frank!"

Fate

She tried to lean coaxingly against his knees, but he stood up; her tears angered him and made him more obstinate. His wife had never got anything from him by tears; quite the reverse. Eva was silly and childish. He could not recognize his spirited daughter—always indefatigable and bright —with whom he had traveled half over the world, in this crushed creature dissolved in woe.

"Stand up, Eva," he said, sternly. "Do not crouch on the floor. You will end by vexing me seriously with your folly. What are you crying for? For nothing, pure foolish imagining. I will have no more of it. You must behave reasonably. Get up, stand up."

She dragged herself to her feet, groaning as she did so, with a white face and clenched hands.

"I can not help it," she said. "It is my nature, I suppose. Have you no pity for your child, even if you do not understand her? Oh, go and speak to him—only a few words, I implore you—I beseech you."

"No, no, no!" he cried, stamping his foot, his face quite red as if from a congestion of rage at all this useless, undefined vexation, and his daughter's folly, and weeping and entreaties, which his obstinacy urged him on no account to indulge. She however rose, looking taller in her despair; her eyes had a strange look as they gazed into her father's.

Fate

"Then you will not speak to Frank? You will not do that much for me?"

"No. It is all nonsense, I tell you. Worry me about it no more."

"Very well. Then, I must do it," she said gravely, as if pronouncing some irrevocable decision. And very slowly, without looking round, without bidding him good-night, she left the room. It was as though Sir Archibald was a total stranger, as though there were no bond of tenderness between her and her father—nothing but the hostility of two antagonistic natures. No; under their superficial affection they had had no feeling in common; they had never really known, never tried to understand each other; she had no sympathy with his old age; he had none with her youth. They were miles asunder; a desert, a pathless waste, lay between them. They dwelt apart as completely as though they were locked up in two shrines, where each worshiped a different God.

"He is my father," thought she, as she went along the passage. "I am his child."

She could not understand it. It was a mystery of nature that scarcely seemed possible. He—her father, she—his child; and yet he could not feel her anguish—could not see that it was anguish—called it folly and fancy. And a vehement longing for her mother rose up in her heart. She would have understood!

Fate

"Mamma, mamma!" she sobbed out. "Oh mamma, come back. Tell me what I can do. Come as a ghost; I will not be afraid of you. I am so forlorn, so miserable—so miserable! Come and haunt me; come, only come!"

In her room, in the darkness, she watched for the ghost. But it came not. The night hung unbroken, like a black curtain, behind which there was nothing but emptiness.

Fate

CHAPTER XVII

WHEN Frank came to call next morning, he at once saw in her face that she was greatly agitated.

"What is the matter, dearest?" he asked.

At first she felt weak. There was something so terrible—and then again so shocking—but she commanded herself; she drew herself up in her pretty self-will, which gave firmness to the child-like enthusiasm and womanly coyness of her nature, like a sterner background against which so much that was soft and tender stood out. And, feeling above all that she stood alone, abandoned by her father, she was determined to be firm.

"Frank, I have no alternative," she began, with the energy of despair. "I must talk matters over with you. Even before you answer me I am almost convinced that I am wrong, and think myself odious; but still I must speak, for I am too unhappy under this—all this. To keep it all to myself in silence is more than I can bear; I can endure it no longer, Frank. I asked papa to speak to you, but he will not. Perhaps he is right; still, it is not kind of him, for now I must do it myself."

Fate

Even in the excited state of mind she was in she loathed this cruel necessity; but she controlled herself and went on:

"That woman—Frank, Frank! That woman—I can think of nothing else!"

"But, dear Eva!"

"Oh! let me speak—I must speak; I see that creature always at my elbow; I smell her perfume; I hear her voice. I can not get it out of my ears." She shuddered violently, and the dreadful thing came over her again, again possessed her; the ghostly hypnotism of that eye, that whisper, that strange magnetic power which her father could not understand. The words she spoke seemed prompted, inspired by that voice; her expression and attitude obeyed the coercion of that gaze. In her inmost soul she felt those eyes as black as night.

"Oh, Frank!" she cried, and the tears came from nervous excitement, and the fear lest she should not have courage to obey these promptings. "I must, I *must* ask you. Why, when you come to see me, are you always so grave and silent, as though you were not happy in my society; why do you evade all direct replies; why do you always tell me that there is nothing the matter? That woman —it is because of her, because you still love her— better, perhaps, than you love me! Because you can not forget her, because she still is a part of

Fate

your life, a large part—perhaps the largest? Oh,
it is such torture, such misery—ever-present misery. And I am not meanly jealous; I never have
been. I quite understand your feeling about her
—the first-comer—though it is dreadful. But you
yourself are too silent, too sad; and when I think
it over I doubt, in spite of myself—Frank, in spite
of myself, I swear to you. But the suspicion forces
itself upon me and overwhelms me! Great God,
why must it be? But, Frank, tell me I am a sim-
pleton to think so, and that she is nothing to you
any longer—nothing at all. You never see her, do
you? Tell me, tell me."

The anguish of her soul as she spoke was elo-
quent in her face, though disfigured with grief,
and pale with the dead whiteness of a faded azalea
blossom; a convulsive pang pinched the corners of
her mouth, and her quivering eyelids; she was
indeed a martyr to her own too vivid fancy.

But he, at this moment, was incapable of seeing
her as a martyr. Her words had roused in him a
surge of fury such as he could remember having
felt occasionally as a child, lashed up as it were
by the blast of a hurricane, drowning every other
feeling, sweeping away every other thought, like
dust before the storm. It came blustering up at the
notion of his honesty being questioned, his perfect
candor, honor, and truth—like a whirlwind of
righteous indignation at such injustice; for in his

own mind he could not conceive of such a doubt, knowing himself to be honest, honorable, and true. His dark gray eyes flashed beneath his deeply knit brows; his words came viciously from between his set teeth, which shone large and white under his mustache, like polished ivory.

"It is inconceivable! Good God, this is monstrous! I have answered you, once for all; I have told you in plain words: 'No—no—no!' And you ask me again and again. Do you think I am a liar? Why? Have you ever seen anything in me to make you think I can lie? I say no, and I mean no! And still you have doubts; still you think and worry over it like an old woman. Why do you not take things as they are? You know the facts; why do you not believe me? I am not sad, I am not gloomy; I am quite happy with you; I love you; I do not doubt you. But you—you!— Believe me, if you go on in this way you will make yourself miserable; and me too, me too!"

She looked at him steadfastly, and her pride rose up to meet his wrath, for his words offended her.

"You need not speak to me in that tone," she answered haughtily. "When I tell you that it is against my will—you hear—in spite of myself, that I have doubts, and that this makes me miserable, you need not take that tone. Have some pity on me, and do not speak like that."

"But, Eva, when I assure you," he began again,

Fate

trembling with rage, which he tried to control, forcing himself to speak gently: "when I assure you."

"You had done so already."

"And you doubt my word?"

"Only in so far as—"

"You disbelieve me?" he roared, quite beside himself.

"Only in so far as that I think you are keeping something back," she cried.

"Something back! What, in Heaven's name?"

His friend's name was on her tongue; but as soon as she thought of Bertie, hesitancy and indecision took possession of her, for she knew not what exactly Bertie had in fact told her. It was always as though Van Maeren had enclosed her in a magic circle, a spell of silence, which made it impossible for her to mention him; and even at this juncture he was an intangible presence, his name an unutterable word, his hints a mere inarticulate jangle.

"What—what?" she gasped in bewilderment. "Oh, I do not know. If only I knew! But you are concealing something from me—and perhaps it is something about her, that woman!"

"But when I tell you that she—"

"No, no," she insisted, confirmed in her imaginings by her offended pride. "I know—I know. You men count such matters as nothing. A thing of the past; it is so all the world over, you say; and what I call something, you call nothing. And so I say there is something—that you are hiding, Frank."

"Eva, I swear—"

"Do not swear to it, for that would be a sin!" she shrieked out, wrought up, in spite of herself, to a paroxysm of insane belief in a thing of which she knew nothing certain. "For I feel it. I feel it here, in me, about me, everywhere!"

He seized her by the wrists, carried away by his rage at her rejecting his asseverations, wounded in his proud consciousness of honor and truthfulness, and amazed at the depth of her infatuated distrust.

"Then you do not believe me," he said, with an oath. "You do not believe me?" And for the second time his tone offended and enraged her. The exposure of their two antagonistic natures, with all their passions and infirmities, brought them into collision.

"No; since you will have it— No!" she cried, and she wrenched herself free from his vise-like grasp with such violence that her slender wrists cracked. "Now you know it: I do not believe you. You are hiding something from me, and it has something to do with that woman. I feel it, and what I feel is to me undeniable. That creature, who dared to speak to you, has taken root in my imagination; I feel her close to me, smell her scent, and am so intensely conscious that there is still something between you and her that I am bold to say to you: 'You lie; you lie for her sake and are cheating me!' "

With a sort of low bellow, which broke from him involuntarily, he rushed at her, clenching his fists, and she mechanically shrank back. But he seized her hands again, enclosing them in his great strong fingers, so that she felt his power through her flesh, in her very bones.

"Oh"—and it was like muttering thunder; "you have no heart—none, that you can say such things to me! You are base, mean, even to think them! 'You feel, and you feel!' Yes. It is your own petty narrowness that you feel. You have nothing in you but base and contemptible incredulity! Your whole nature is mean! Everything is at an end between us; I have nothing more to do with you. I was mistaken in you."

He flung her off, on to a sofa. There she remained, staring up at the ceiling, with wide-open eyes. At the moment she was startled rather than angry, and did not fully understand the state of things. Her overwrought brain was bewildered; she knew not what had happened.

For a minute he stood looking at her. His lips wore a sneer of contempt, and his eyes, half closed in scorn, glanced over her prostrate form. He saw

how pretty she was; her graceful figure, stretched
on the Turkish pillows, revealed the soft lines of
its supple, girlish mold through the clinging folds
of a thin pale green material; her hair, which had
come loose, hung to the floor, like the red-gold
fleece of some rare wild creature; her bosom heaved
with spasmodic rapidity. She lay there like a
ravished maid, flung aside in a fit of passion. He
saw all the charms that he had forfeited; deep
wrath sprang up in him, a wild longing for the
happiness he had lost; but his injured honor ousted
regrets and longing. He turned away and left her
there.

She remained on the same spot, in the same attitude. She was full of obscure wonderment; darkness had fallen on her soul, as though, after being
entrapped by falsehood, blindfolded by doubt, she
had been led into a labyrinth and then suddenly
released—her eyes unbound—in a dark chamber.
Her soul indeed seemed to have bled to death; she
could not yet know how deeply it was wounded,
and in spite of her intolerable grief she still thought
only of the darkness about her.

"How strange," she whispered. "But why? In
Heaven's name, why?"

Fate

CHAPTER XVIII

AFTER this there was a month of peace. A sudden calm had fallen on them both, full, for both alike, of silent, bitter grief. And, with it all, the insignificant commonplace of ordinary life, and the recurring, monotonous tasks of every day.

Even Bertie found himself breathing this strange, stagnant air. He wondered greatly what could have occurred. How simply, how easily, things had worked themselves out! He? No, he had done nothing; he could have done nothing. Events had merely followed each other. What had come about was the inevitable. And the possibility of a life free from care again lay before him; an eternity of comfort and wealth with Westhove, for whom he felt his old affection revive with the glow almost of a passion, now that Frank, severed from Eva, though blaming himself indeed, needed consolation and sympathy. And Bertie's low, unctuous tones were full of sympathy. Oh, the dark melancholy of the first few days, the terrible grief of wondering, when now, his indignation cold, Frank asked himself, as Eva had asked herself, Why? Why had this happened? What had he done? What had brought it about? And he could not see, could not understand; it was like a book out of which leaves have been torn so as to spoil the sense. He could comprehend neither himself and his fury, nor Eva and her doubts. All life seemed to him a riddle. For hours together he would sit gazing out of the window, staring at the opaque dulness of the London fog, his eye fixed on that riddle. He rarely went out, but sat dreaming in White-Rose Cottage, which was lonely and quiet enough in its remote suburb. An enervating indifference possessed his stalwart frame; for the first time in his life he saw himself in a true light, and detected the vacillation and weakness deep down in his being, like a lymphatic stream traversing his sanguine physical vigor. He saw himself, as a mere child in resistance to the storm of rage, the blast of fury which had swept away his happiness. And his suffering was so terrible that he could not entirely comprehend it; it seemed too all-embracing for the human mind.

These were days of dreary gloom which they spent together; Frank too dejected to go out of doors, Bertie creeping about very softly under the pressure of a vague dread and indefinable dissatisfaction. He felt Frank's friendship reviving, and, flattered by this revival, was conscious of a sentiment of pity, almost of sympathy; he tried to rouse Frank from his moodiness, and talked of a supper party—with ladies—on the old pattern. He made plans for going away, here or there, for a few days. He tried to persuade Westhove to take to work, mentioning the names of various great engineers who were to be found in London. But everything fell dead against Frank's obdurate melancholy, everything was swallowed up in the dark cloud of his dejection, which seemed incapable of more than one idea—one self-reproach, one grief. And the only solace of his life was always to have Bertie at his side; a closer intimacy to which Van Maeren himself was no less prompted, now that he had gained his selfish ends, having no further fear of impending poverty, and seeing always by him a consuming sorrow. Had he not rejected the notion that he had been the cause of it all? And had he not, during his late existence as an idle bachelor, become so superfine a being that he felt a craving for the vague delights of sympathy; nothing more than sympathy, since no great and noble love, no strong and generous friendship could breathe in the complicated recesses of his soul, for lack of room and fresh air in those narrow cells built up on strange fallacies, and since love and friendship must pine and die there, like a lion in a boudoir.

Thus it was that he could still feel for Frank. could lay his hands on his shoulders and try to comfort him, could find words of affection—new on his lips—and unwonted phrases of consolation or cheering. Women, he would say, were so narrow-minded; they were nothing, they loved nothing, they were a mere delusion; no man should ever make himself miserable for a woman. There was nothing like friendship, which women could not even understand, and never felt for each other; a passion of sympathy, the noble joy of affinity and agreement. And he believed what he said, sunning himself in Platonism with catlike complacency, just as he basked in material ease and comfort, rejoicing in his raptures of friendship, and admiring himself for his lofty ideals.

But Frank's love for Eva had been, and was still, so absorbing, that he erelong saw through this effete and decrepit devotion, and thenceforward it afforded him no solace. His depression wrapped him in darker folds. He forced himself to recall exactly everything that had happened; what Eva had said, what he had replied. And he laid all the blame on himself, exonerating Eva for her doubts; he cursed his own temper, his barbarous violence to a woman—and to her! What was to be done? Parted—parted forever! It was a fearful thought that he might never see her again, that she could be nothing henceforth in his life. Could it be no otherwise? Was ail lost? Irrevocably?

No, no, no; the desperate denial rose up within

him; he would triumph over circumstances; he would win back his happiness.

And she? How was she? Was she, too, suffering? Did she still doubt him, or had his vehemence, notwithstanding its brutality, made his innocence clear? But if it were so, if she no longer doubted him—and how could she?—good heavens, how wretched she must be! Grieving over her want of trust, with self-accusation even more terrible than his own—for his wrath had at any rate been justifiable, and her suspicions were not.

Was it so? Or was she, on the contrary, stricken almost to death, perhaps, by his cruelty, or filled with contempt for his lack of power to control his anger, which was like some raging wild beast? How was she? What was her mood? A passionate desire to know pierced his heart now and again like a sword-thrust; to go to her, to pray for pardon, for restoration to the happiness he had thrown away, as he had flung her from him on that sofa. She would never admit him to her presence after so great an insult. But he might write. Of course, a letter! His heart leaped with joy. What bliss to grovel, on paper, in the dust, at her feet; to humble himself in penitential prayers for mercy, and adoring words, while asserting his dignity in the pride of his truth, and his anguish under her doubts! She would hearken, as a Madonna to a sinner; he would recover his lost happiness!

Fate

And he tried to compose his letter, thrilling with the effort to find words, which still did not seem fervent or humble enough.

He spent a whole day over his task, polishing his phrases as a poet does a sonnet. And when at last it was finished he felt refreshed in spirit, with renewed hopes—a complete resurrection. He was convinced that his letter would remove every mis-understanding between him and Eva.

In the highest spirits he betook himself to Van Maeren, told his friend of the step he had taken, and all he hoped for. He spoke eagerly; his very voice was changed.

Bertie leaned back in his chair, rather grave and pale; but he controlled himself so far as to smile in answer to Westhove's smile, and he agreed in his anticipations in words to which he vainly strove to give a ring of conviction.

"To be sure, of course, everything must come right again," he muttered; and the perspiration stood on his forehead under his chestnut curls.

Fate

CHAPTER XIX

BUT an hour later, alone in his room that evening, he walked to and fro with such seething agitation as set every nerve quivering in his slight frame, as a storm tosses a rowboat. His soft features were distorted to a hideous expression of malignancy, with rage at his own impotence, and he strode up and down, up and down, like a beast in a cage, clenching his fists. Then it was for this that he had elaborated his tastes, had sharpened and polished all his natural gifts, and had directed all the powers of his mind like a battery charged with some mysterious fluid, on the secrets of a girl's love and life! A single letter, a few pages of tender words, and the whole work would be destroyed! For now, in his wrath, he suddenly saw and prided himself on the fact; he saw that he—very certainly he—had guided events to sever Frank and Eva. How could he even for a moment have doubted it?

And it was all to come to naught! Never, never! No, a thousand times, no! Awful, and infinitely far as the horizon, the perspective of life

Fate

yawned before him—the dead level of poverty, the barren desert in which he must pine and perish of hunger. And in his horror of treading that wilderness every sinew of his lax resolve seemed strained to the verge of snapping.

He must take steps forthwith. An idea flashed through his brain like the zigzag of forked lightning. Yes; that was his only course; the simplest and most obvious means, a mere stroke of villainy —as conventionality would term it. . . . No need here for any elaborate psychological *pros* and *cons;* they were never of any use; they got entangled in their own complications. Simply a theatrical *coup.*

He took his hat and crept quietly out of the house, with a sneer of contempt, of scorn for himself, that he should have fallen so low. It was half-past ten. He hailed a cab, and laughed to hear the melodramatic sound of his own voice as he gave the driver Sir Archibald's address— the voice of a stage traitor. Then he shrank into a corner of the vehicle, his shoulders up to his ears, his eyes half closed and gazing out through the dim mystery of the night. Deadly melancholy lurked at the bottom of his soul.

He got out near Sir Archibald's house, walked a few yards to the door, and rang—and the minutes he waited in the darkness before the closed house seemed an eternity of intolerable misery, of horror, aversion, loathing of himself. His lips were pinched into a grimace of disgust.

A man-servant opened the door with a look of surprise at the belated visitor, a surprise which gave way to an impertinent stare when he saw that Van Maeren was alone, without Westhove. He bowed with insolent irony, and held the door wide open with exaggerated servility, for Bertie to enter.

"I must speak with you at once," said Bertie, coolly, "at once and alone."

The man looked at him, but said nothing.

"You can do me a service. I need your assistance—pressingly. Can I say two words to you without being seen by any one?"

"Now?" said the servant.

"Yes, now; without delay."

"Will you come in—into the servants' hall?"

"No, no. Come out and walk up and down with me. And speak low."

"I can not leave the house yet. The old man will be going to bed in an hour or so, and then I can join you in the street."

"Then I will wait for you; opposite, by the Park railings. You will be sure to come? I will make it worth your while." The footman laughed, a loud, brazen laugh, which rang through the hall, filling Bertie with alarm. "Then you are a gentleman now? And pretty flush, eh?"

Fate

"Yes," said Van Maeren hoarsely. "Then you will come?"

"Yes, yes. In an hour or more, fully an hour. Wait for me. But if I am to do anything for you, you will have to fork out, you know; and fork out handsomely too!"

"All right, all right," said Bertie. "But I hope you will not fail me. I count on your coming, mind."

The door was ruthlessly shut. He walked up and down for a very long time in the cold and damp. The chill pierced to his very marrow, while the twinkling gas lamps stared at him through the gray mist like watery eyes. He waited, pacing the pavement for an hour—an hour and a half—perishing of fatigue and cold, like a beggar without a shelter. Still he waited, shivering as he walked, his hands in his pockets, his eyes dull with self-contempt, staring out of his white face at the dark square of the door, which still remained shut.

Fate

CHAPTER XX

WHEN, after a few days of anxious expectancy, Frank still had no answer from Eva, he wrote a second time; and although the first bloom of his revived hopes was already dying, he started whenever the bell rang, and would go to the letter-box in the front door; his thoughts were constantly busy with picturing the messenger who was walking up the road with his happiness—wrapped up in an envelope. And he would imagine what Eva's answer might be: just a few lines—somewhat cool, perhaps—in her large bold English hand, on the scented, ivory-laid paper she always used, with her initials crossed in pink and silver in one corner.

How long she took to write that answer! Was she angry? Or could she not make up her mind how to word her forgiveness; was she elaborating her letter as he had elaborated his? And the days went by while he waited for that note. When he was at home, he pictured the postman coming nearer and nearer, now only four—three—two doors away; now he would ring—and he listened; but the bell did not sound, or, if it did, it was not

Fate

by reason of the letter. When he was out, he would be electrified by the thought that the letter must be lying at home and he hurried back to White-Rose Cottage, looked in the letter-box, and then in the sitting-room. But he never found it, and the intolerable emptiness of the place where he looked for it made him swear and stamp with rage.

Twice had he written—two letters—and yet she gave no sign! And he could think of no cause in his ardent expectancy which made him regard it as the most natural thing that she should reply at once. Still he lived on this waiting. The reply must come; it could not be otherwise. His brain held no other thought than: It is coming—it will come to-day. All life was void and flat, but it could be filled by just one letter. Day followed day, and there was no change.

"I have had no answer yet from Eva," he said, in a subdued tone to Bertie, as feeling himself humiliated, disgraced by her determined silence, mocked at in his illusory hopes.

"Not yet?" said Bertie; and a mist of melancholy glistened in his black velvety eyes. A weight indeed lay on his mind; he sighed deeply and frequently. He really was unhappy. What he had done was so utterly base. But it was all Frank's fault. Why, now that he was parted from Eva, could he not forget his passion; why could

Fate

he not find sufficient comfort in the sweets of
friendship? How delightful it might have been
to live on together, a happy pair of friends, under
the calm blue sky of brotherhood, in the golden
bliss of perfect sympathy, with no woman to dis-
turb it. Thus he romanced, consciously working
up his friendly, compassionate feeling toward
Frank to a sort of frenzy, in the hope of comforting himself a little, of forgetting his foul deed, of
convincing himself that he was magnanimous;
nay, that in spite of that little deception, he now
more than ever since he was sunk in the mire,
really longed for a high ideal. It was all Frank's
fault. And yet, was Frank to blame because he
could not forget Eva? No, no. That was all
fatality. No one was to blame for that. That was
the act of Fate.

"Yes, that is certain!" thought he. "But why
have we brains to think with, and why do we feel
pain, if we can do nothing to help ourselves? Why
are we not plants or stones? Why should this
vast, useless universe exist at all? And why, why
did nothingness cease to be? How peaceful, how
delightfully peaceful, that would be!"

He stood, as it were, before the sealed portals of
the great Enigma, suddenly amazed and horrified
at himself. Good God! How had he come to this;
how was it that nowadays he was always thinking
of such things? Had he ever had such notions

Fate

in America, when he was toiling and tramping in his daily slavery? Had he not then regarded himself as a gross materialist, caring for nothing but plenty of good food and unbroken peace? And now, when he had long experience of such material comforts, now he felt as though his nerves had been spun finer and finer to mere silken threads, thrilling and quivering under one emotion after another, vibrating like the invisible aerial pulsations which are irresistibly transmitted, with a musical murmur, along the telephone wires overhead. How had he come by all this philosophy, the blossom of his idle hours? And in his bewilderment he tried to recall his youth, and remember whether he had then had this predisposition to thought, whether he had then had any books which had impressed him deeply; tried to picture his parents, and whether this might be hereditary. And he—he—had handed round coffee-cups in New York! Was he not after all happier in those days and freer from care? Or was it only that "distance lent enchantment to the view," the distance of so few years?

Fate

CHAPTER XXI

WHEN Frank, after a few days of death-in-life patience, had still received no answer, he wrote to Sir Archibald. Still the same silence. He poured out his grief to Bertie in bitter complaint, no longer humble, but full of wrath like an enraged animal, and yet half woful at the ill-feeling shown by Eva and her father. Was it not enough that he had three times craved forgiveness? Had Eva cared for him in fact so little, that when he groveled at her feet she could find no word even to tell him that all was at an end?

"I can not now remember all I said," he told Bertie, as he paced the room with long, equal, and determined steps. "But I must have been hard upon her. God help me, I can never govern my speech! And I seized her, I recollect, so, by the arms. And then I came away. I was too furious. I ought not to have done it; but I can not keep cool, I can not."

"Frank, I wish you could get over it," said Bertie soothingly, from the depths of his armchair. "There is nothing now to be done. It is very sad that it should have happened so, but you must throw it off."

"Throw it off! Were you ever in love with a woman?"

"Certainly."

"Then you must know something of it— But you could never love any one much; it is not in your nature. You love yourself too well."

"That may be; but at any rate I love you, and I can not bear to see you thus, Frank. Get over it! They seem to have taken the whole business so ill that there is nothing more to be done. I wish you would only see that, and submit to the inevitable. Try to live for something else. Can there be no other woman in the world for you? Perhaps there is another. A man does not perish so for love. You are not a girl—girls do so."

He gazed at Frank with such a magnetic light in his eyes that Westhove fancied there was a great truth in his words; and Bertie's last reproof reminded him of his vacillation, his miserable weakness, which lay beneath his manly and powerful exterior like an insecure foundation. Still he clung to his passionate longings, his vehement craving for the happiness he had lost.

"You can not possibly judge of the matter," he retorted impatiently, trying to escape from Van Maeren's eye. "You never *did* love a woman, though you may say so. Why should not everything come right again? What has happened after all? What have I done? I fell into a violent, vulgar rage? What then? Is that so unpardonable in the person you love? But perhaps —I say, can I have addressed the letters wrongly?"

During a few seconds there was a weight of silence in the room, an atmosphere of lead. Then Van Maeren said—and his voice had a tender, coaxing tone:

"If you had written but once, I might think it possible; but three letters, to the same house—it is scarcely possible."

"I will go myself and call," said Westhove. "Yes, yes, I will go myself."

"What are you saying?" asked Bertie dreamily. He was still under the influence of that heavy moral atmosphere; he had not quite understood, not grasped the idea. "What was it you said?" he repeated.

"I shall go myself and call at the house," Frank reiterated.

"At what house? Where?"

"Why, at the Rhodeses'—on Eva. Are you daft?"

But Bertie rose to his feet, and his eyes glittered in his pale face like black diamonds with a hundred facets.

"What to do there?" he said with a convulsive effort in his throat to keep his voice calm

Fate

"To talk to her and set matters straight; I can not bear it. It has gone on too long."

"You are a fool!" said Van Maeren shortly.

"Why am I a fool?"

"Why are you a fool? You have not a grain of self-respect. Do you really think of going there?"

"Yes, of course."

"I consider it absurd," said Bertie.

"All right," said Frank, "pray think so. I myself can see that it is very weak of me. But, good God! I can hold out no longer. I love her so; I was so happy; life was so sweet; and now; now, by my own fault! I do not care what you think it. Absurd or not, I mean to go all the same."

In his distress of mind he had thrown himself into a chair, and every muscle of his features was quivering with agitation. But he went on:

"I do not know what it is that I feel; I am so unhappy, so deeply, deeply wretched. Never in my life had I known what it was to feel so content, in such harmonious equilibrium of soul as when I was with Eva; at least so it seems to me now. And now it is all at an end, and everything seems aimless. I no longer know why I live and move and eat and have my being! Why should I take all that trouble, and then have this misery into the bargain? I might just as well be dead. You see, that is why I mean to call there. And

Fate

if things do not come right then, well, I shall make an end of myself! Yes, yes, I shall make an end of myself."

Crushed by the burden of life, he lay back in his chair, with his features set, his great limbs stretched out in their useless strength, all his power undermined by the mysterious inertia which gnawed it away like a worm. Before him stood Van Maeren, drawn to his full height in the energy of despair, and his flashing eyes darting sparks of fire. He laid his tremulous hands on Westhove's shoulders, feeling their massive breadth, heavy and strong. A reaction electrified him with something like defiance; he scorned this man of might in his love-sickness. But above all, oh, above all, he felt himself being dragged down to the lowest deep; and it was with the tenacity of a parasitic growth that he clung to Frank, setting his fingers into his shoulders.

"Frank," he began, almost hoarsely, "just listen to me. You are making yourself ill. You talk like a fool, and then you cry out just like a baby. You must get over it. Show a little more pluck. Do not mar your whole life by these foolish lamentations. And what about, when all is said and done, what about? All because a girl has ceased to love you. Do you place your highest hopes of happiness in a girl? They are creatures without brains or heart; superficial and vain, whipped up to a froth—mere windy nothingness. And you would kill yourself for that? Heaven above, man! It is impossible— I do not know what it is to love a woman, eh? But you do not know what trouble and misery are. You fancy that all the woes on earth have come upon you. And it is nothing, after all, but a little discomfort, a little wounded conceit perhaps—it will be no worse. If I had made away with myself at every turn of ill-luck, I should have been dead a thousand times. But I pulled through, you see. How can you be such a coward? Eva has shown you very plainly that she does not want to have anything more to say to you; and you would seek her once more! Suppose she were to show you the door? What then? If you do such a thing, if you go to her, you will be so mean in my eyes, so weak, so cowardly, so childish, such a fool, such a damned fool, that you may go to the devil for aught I care!"

He cleared his throat as if he were actually sick, and turned away with a queer, light-headed feeling in his brain.

Westhove said nothing, torn in his mind between two impulses. He was no longer clear as to his purpose, quite bewildered by the false voice in his ear—in his soul. There was something factitious in Bertie's speech, a false ring which Frank could not detect, though he was conscious of it; and the voice of his own desires rang false too, with jarring, unresolved chords, which jangled inharmoniously against each other. He had completely lost his head, but he sat silent for some time, till at length he repeated, with sullen obstinacy:

"All right. I do not care a pin. I shall go all the same."

But Bertie began again, with honeyed smoothness this time, seating himself on the floor, as was his wont when he was out of luck, on the fur rug before the fire, resting his throbbing head against a chair.

"Come, Frank, get this out of your mind. You never meant that you would really go. You are at heart too proud and too brave to think of it seriously. Pull yourself together. Have you forgotten everything? Did not Eva tell you that she did not believe your word, that you were false to her, that you still were friends with that other girl, and that she knew it? To tell you the truth, I observed from the first how suspicious she was, and I did not think it becoming in a young lady; I did not think it quite—quite nice— To be sure, that evening at the Lyceum, it did look as if there was something in it. Still, when you assured her that it was at an end, it seems to me quite monstrous that she did not believe you then. You can not possibly mean what you say when you speak of seeking her again. Of course it makes no difference to me; go by all means, for what I care;

but I should regard it as such folly, such utter folly—"

And still Frank sat speechless, lost, with the bewildering jangle still in his brain.

"And you will take the same view of it if you only think it over. Think it over, Frank."

"I will," said Frank, gloomily.

Bertie went on, flattering his manly courage, and it sounded like bells in Frank's ears: pride, pluck; pride, pluck: only the bells were cracked. And yet the jingle soothed him. Did he at this moment love Eva? Or was it all over, had she killed his love by her doubt? Pride, pluck; pride, pluck. He could not tell—alas! he could not tell.

With a movement like a caress, Bertie crept nearer, laid his head on the arm of Westhove's chair, and clasped his hands about his knees, looking, in the dusk and firelight, like a supple panther; and his eyes gleamed like a panther's, black and flame-colored.

"Speak, Frank; I can not bear to see you like this. I care for you so much, though perhaps it does not seem so to you just now, and though I have my own way of showing it. Oh, I know very well that you sometimes think me ungrateful. But you do not know me; I am really devoted to you. I never loved my father, nor any woman, nor even myself, as I do you. I could do anything in the world for you, and that is a great deal for me to say. I say, Frank, I will not have you look so. Let us leave London; let us travel, or go to live somewhere else—in Paris or Vienna. Yes, let us go to Vienna—that is a long way off; or to America, to San Francisco; or to Australia—wherever you choose. The world is wide, and you may see so many things that you will get fresh ideas. Or let us make an expedition to the interior of Africa. I should enjoy seeing such a savage country, and I am stronger than I look; I am tough. Let us wander about a great deal, and go through a great deal—great bodily fatigue. Don't you think it must be splendid to cut your way through the impenetrable bush? Oh, yes, let us bathe our souls in nature, in fresh air, and space, and health."

"Well, well," Frank grumbled, "we will go away. We will travel. But I can not do it comfortably: I have very little money. I spent so much last year."

"Oh, but we will be economical; what need have we of luxury? I, at any rate, can do without it."

"Very well," Frank muttered again. "We will do it cheaply."

Then they were silent for a time. In the twilight, Frank by some slight movement touched one of Bertie's hands. He suddenly grasped it, squeezed it almost to crushing, and said in a low voice:

"Good old fellow! Dear, good fellow!"

Fate

CHAPTER XXII

CAN he have gone there? thought Van Maeren as he sat at home alone the next evening, and did not know with what purpose Westhove had gone out. Well, he would sit up for him; there was nothing else to be done. Just a few days to arrange matters and then they would be off, away from London. Oh, what a luckless wretch he thought himself. All this villainy for the sake of mere material comfort, of idleness, and wealth, which, as he was slowly beginning to discover, had all become a matter of indifference to him. Oh! for the Bohemian liberty of his vagabond life in the States, free, unshackled; his pockets now full of dollars and again empty, absolutely empty! He felt quite homesick for it; it struck him as an enviable existence of careless independence as compared with his present state of vacuous ease and servility. How greatly he was changed. Formerly he had been unfettered indeed by conventional rules, but free from any great duplicity; and now, his mind had been cultivated, but was sunk in a depth of baseness. And what for? To enable him to hold fast that which no longer had any value in his eyes. No value? Why, then, did he not cut his way out of his own net, to go away, in poverty; and write a single word to Frank and Eva to bring them together again? It was still in his power to do this.

He thought of it, but smiled at the thought; it was impossible, and yet he could not see wherein the impossibility lay. But it *was* impossible, it was a thing which could not be done. It was illogical, full of dark difficulties, a thing that could never come about for mysterious reasons of Fatality, which, indeed, he did not clearly discern, but accepted as unanswerable.

He was musing in this vein, alone that evening, when Annie, the housekeeper, came to tell him that some one wanted to speak with him.

"Who is it?"

She did not know, so he went into the sitting-room, where he found Sir Archibald's footman, with his big nose and ugly, shifty, gray eyes, like a bird's, twinkling in his terra-cotta face, which was varied by blue tracts of shorn whisker and beard. He was out of his livery, and dressed like a gentleman, in a light overcoat and a felt hat, with a cane and gloves.

"What brings you here?" said Van Maeren, shortly, with a scowl. "I have always told you that I would not have you come to the house. You have no complaint to make of me, I suppose?"

Fate

Oh, no, he had no complaint to make, he had only come to call on an old friend—such a swell! Bertie would remember the times they had had in New York. They had been waiters together, pals at the same hotel. Rum chance, eh, that they should run up against each other in London? It was a small world; you were always running up against some one wherever you might go. You couldn't keep out of any one's way; in fact, if it was God's will you should meet a feller you couldn't keep out of that feller's way, and then you might sometimes be able to do him a good turn. . . . There had been some letters written —and he scraped his throat—inconvenient letters. Sixty quid down for two letters to the young woman, that was the bargain. Life was hard; to get a little fun now and then in London cost a deal of money. And now there was a third letter, in the same hand—dear, dear, whose could it be now?—addressed to the old man. He did not want to be too hard on an old pal, but he had come just to ask whether that letter too was of any value. He had it with him.

"Then give it here," stammered Van Maeren, as pale as death, holding out his hand.

Ay, but thirty sovs. was too little, a mere song. This letter was to the old man, and was worth more, and, to tell the truth, his old friend was hard up, desperately hard up. Bertie was a gentleman who could throw the money about, and he had a noble heart. He would never leave an old pal in the lurch. The devil's in it, we must help each other in this world. Say a hundred?

"You are a rascal!" cried Bertie. "We had agreed on thirty pounds. I have not a hundred pounds; I am not rich."

Well, of course he knew that; but Mr. Westhove, no doubt, gave his friend sixpence now and then, and Mr. Westhove was made of money. Come, come, Mr. Van Maeren must think it over; he really should do something for an old pal, and a hundred pounds was not the whole world after all.

"I have not a hundred pounds at this moment, I assure you," said Bertie, huskily, from a parched throat, and shaking as if in an ague fit.

Well, he would come again then, by and by. He would take great care of the letter.

"Hand over the letter. I will give you the money another time."

But his "old pal" laughed cheerfully. No, no—given is given. They might trust each other, but it should be give and take—the letter for the hundred pounds down.

"But I will not have you coming here again. I will not have it, I tell you."

All right. There was no difficulty on that score. His swell friend might bring it himself. To-morrow?

Fate

"Yes, to-morrow without fail. And now go; for God's sake, go!"

He pushed his demon out of the house, promising him, to-morrow—to-morrow evening. Then he called up Annie, and vehemently asked her whether she knew the man.

"Who was the fellow?" he roughly inquired, like a gambler who plays a high trump at a critical point of the game.

She, however, did not know, and was surprised that Mr. Van Maeren should not have known him. Had he been troublesome?

"Yes, a beggar, a regular beggar."

"He was dressed quite like a gentleman, too."

"Be more careful for the future," said Bertie, "and let no one into the house."

Fate

CHAPTER XXIII

HE sat up that evening till Frank came home. As he sat alone he wept; for hours he sobbed passionately, miserably, till, in the slightly built little villa, Annie and her husband might have heard him, till his head felt like a drum, and bursting with throbbing pain. He fairly cried in irrepressible wretchedness, and his sobs shook his little body like a rhythm of agony. Oh, how could he get out of this slough? Kill himself? How could he live on in such wretchedness? And again and again he looked about him for a weapon; his hands clutched his throat like a vice. But he had not the courage—at least not at that moment, for as he clenched his fingers an unendurable pain mounted to his already aching head. And he wept all the more bitterly at finding himself too weak to do it.

It was one in the morning. Frank must surely come in soon.

He looked in the glass, and saw a pale, purple-gray face with swollen, wet eyes, and thick blue veins on the temples pulsating visibly under the transparent skin. Frank must not see him thus. And yet he must know—and he must ask—

He went up to his room, undressed, and got shivering into bed; but he did not go to sleep. He lay listening for the front door to open. At half-past two Westhove came in. Good God! If he had gone to the Rhodeses'. No, no, he must have been at the club; he went straight upstairs to bed. Annie and her husband locked up the house; there was a noise of bolts and locks, the clank of metal bars.

Half an hour later Bertie rose. Now it would be dark in Frank's room—otherwise he would have seen that purple pallor. Out into the passage. Tap. "Frank."

"Hallo! Come in."

In he went. Westhove was in bed; no light but the night-light; Bertie, with his back to the glimmer. Now, would Frank mention the Rhodeses? No. He asked, What was up? And Van Maeren began.

There was an urgent matter he must lay before his friend—some old debts he had remembered, which he must pay before they went away. He was so vexed about it; it was really taking advantage of Frank's kindness. Could Frank give him the money?

"My dear fellow, I have run completely dry.

Fate

I have only just enough left to pay for our passage to Buenos Ayres. How much do you want?"

"A hundred pounds."

"A hundred pounds! I assure you I do not know where to lay my hand on the money. Do you want it now, on the spot? Can you not put it off? Or can you not do with a bill?"

"No. I must have money down, hard cash."

"Well, wait a bit. Perhaps I can find a way—Yes, I will manage it somehow. I will see about it to-morrow."

"To-morrow morning?"

"Are you in such a deuce of a hurry? Well, all right; I will find it somehow. But now go to bed, for I am sleepy; we made a night of it. To-morrow I am sure I can help you. And, at any rate, I will not leave you in a fix; that you may rely on. But you are a troublesome boy. Do you hear? Only the other day you had thirty pounds, and then, again, thirty more!"

For a minute Van Maeren stood rigid, a dark mass against the dim gleam of the night-light. Then he went up to the bed, and, falling on his knees, laid his head on the coverlet and fairly sobbed.

"I say, are you ill? Are you gone crazy?" asked Westhove. "What on earth ails you?"

No, he was not crazy, but only so grieved to take advantage of Frank's good nature, especially if his

Fate

friend was himself in difficulties. They were such shameful debts—he would rather not tell him what for. Debts outstanding from a time when for a few days he had disappeared. Frank knew, didn't he?"

"Old sins to pay for, eh? Well, behave better for the future. We will set it all right to-morrow. Make no more noise, and go to bed. I am dead sleepy; we all had as much as we could carry. Come, get up, I say."

Van Maeren rose, and, taking Westhove's hand tried to thank him.

"There, that will do—go to bed, I say."

And he went. In his own room he presently, through the wall, heard Frank snoring. He remained sitting on the edge of his bed. Once more his fingers gripped his throat—tighter—tighter. But it hurt him—made his head ache.

"Great God!" he thought. "Is it possible that I should be the thing I am?"

Fate

CHAPTER XXIV

A LIFE of wandering for two years and more, of voyages from America to Australia, from Australia back to Europe; painfully restless, finding no new aims in life, no new reason for their own existence, no new thing in the countries they traversed or in the various atmospheres they breathed. A life at first without the struggle for existence, dragged out by each under the weight of his own woe; with many regrets, but no anxiety as to the material burden of existence. But presently there was the growing dread of that material burden, the unpleasant consciousness that there was no more money coming out from home, month after month; disagreeable transactions with bankers in distant places, constant letter-writing to and fro; in short, the almost total evaporation of a fortune of which too much had long since been dissipated in golden vapor. Then they saw the necessity of looking about them for means of subsistence, and they had taken work in factories, assurance offices, brokers' warehouses, and what not, simply to keep their heads above water in this life which they found so aimless and wretched.

Fate

They had known hours of bitter anguish, and many long days of poverty, with no escape, and the remembrance of White-Rose Cottage. Still, they had felt no longing for White-Rose Cottage again. Gradually yielding to indifference and sullen patience, their fears for the future and struggles to live were the outcome of natural, inherited instinct, rather than of spontaneous impulse and personal desire.

And even in this gloomy indifference Van Maeren had one comforting reflection, one delicate pleasure, exquisite and peculiar, as a solace to his self-contempt; the consolation of knowing that now that Westhove had known some buffeting of fortune, now that they had to work for their bread, he had never felt impelled to leave his friend to his fate or desert him as soon as the game was up.

The impulse to abandon Frank had never risen in his soul, and he was glad of it; glad that, when it occurred to him afterward as a possibility, it was merely as a notion, with which he had no concern, and which was no part of himself. No; he had stuck by Frank; partly perhaps as a result of his cat-like nature and because he clung to his place at Frank's side; but not for that alone. There was something ideal in it, some little sentiment. He liked the notion of remaining faithful to a man who had not a cent left in the world.

Fate

They had worked together, sharing the toil and the pay with brotherly equality.

Two long years. And now they were back in Europe; avoiding England and returning to their native land, Holland—Amsterdam and The Hague. A strange longing had grown up in them both to see once more the places they had quitted so long before, bored by their familiarity, to see the wider world; to drag home their broken lives, as though they hoped there to find a cure, a miraculous balm, to console them for existence. They had scraped together some little savings, and might take a few months of summer holiday by thriftily spending their handful of cash. So they had taken lodgings in a villa at Scheveningen—a little house to the left of the Orange Hotel, looking out over the sea; and the sea had become a changeful background for their lazy summer fancies, for they did not care to wander away amid the bustle of the Kurhaus and the sands. Frank would sit for hours on the balcony, in a cane chair, his legs on the railing, the blue smoke of his cigar curling up in front of his nose; and then he felt soothed, free from all acute pain, resigned to his own uselessness; though with a memory now and again of the past, and of a sorrow which was no longer too keen. And then, stiff with sitting still, he would play a game of quoits or hockey, or fence a little with Bertie, whom he had taught to use the foils. He looked

Fate

full of health, was stouter than of yore, with a fine high color under his clear, tanned skin, a mild gravity in his bright gray eyes, and sometimes a rather bitter curl under his sheeny yellow mustache.

But Bertie suffered more; and as he looked out over the semicircle of ocean and saw the waters break with their endless rollers of blue and green and gray and violet and pearly iridescence— the vaulted sky above, full of endless cloud scenery, sweeping or creeping masses of opaque gray or white, silvery pinions, dappled feathers, drifts of down-like sky-foam—he fancied that his Fate was coming up over the sea. It was coming closer— irresistibly closer. And he watched its approach; he felt it so intensely that sometimes his whole being seemed to be on the alert while he sat motionless in his cane chair, with his eyes fixed on the barren waste of waters.

Fate

CHAPTER XXV

THUS it happened that, sitting here one day, he saw on the shore below, between the tufts of yellow broom growing on the sand-hills, two figures coming toward him, a man and a woman, like finely drawn silhouettes in Indian ink against the silver sea. A pang suddenly shot through his frame, from his heart to his throat—to his temples. But the salt reek came up to him and roused his senses with a freshness that mounted to his brain, so that, in spite of the shock, it remained quite clear, as if filled with a rarer atmosphere. He saw everything distinctly, down to the subtlest detail of hue and line: the silver-gray curve of the horizon, like an enormous glittering, liquid eye, with mother-of-pearl tints, broken by the tumbling crests of the waves, and hardly darker than the spread of sky strewn with a variously gray fleece of rent and raveled clouds; to the right, one stucco façade of the Kurhaus, looking with stupid dignity at the sea out of its staring window-eyes; further away, by the water's edge, the fishing boats, like large walnut-shells, with filmy veils of black netting hanging from the masts, each boat with

Fate

its little flag playfully waving and curling in the breeze; and on the terrace and the strand, among a confused crowd of yellow painted chairs, a throng of summer visitors like a great stain of pale water-color, in gay but delicate tints. He could see quite clearly—here a rent in the red sail of a boat, there a ribbon fluttering from a basket-chair, and again a seagull on the shore swooping to snatch something out of the surf. He noted all these little details, minute and motley trifles, bright specks in the expanse of sky and ocean, and very visible in the subdued light of a sunless day. And those two silhouettes—a man and a woman—grew larger, came nearer, along the sands till they were just opposite to him.

He knew them at once by their general appearance—the man by a peculiar gesture of raising his hat and wiping his forhead, the lady by the way she carried her parasol, the stick resting on her shoulder while she held the point of one of the ribs. And, recognizing them, he had a singular light-headed sensation, as though he would presently be floating dizzily out of his chair, and swept away over the sea. He fell back, feeling strangely weary, and dazzling sparks danced before his fixed gaze like glittering notes of interrogation. What was to be done? Could he devise some ingenious excuse and try to tempt Frank to leave the place, to flee? Oh! how small

Fate

the world was! Was it for this that they had wandered over the globe, never knowing any rest—to meet, at their very first halting-place, the two beings he most dreaded? Was this accident or Fatality? Yes, Fatality! But then—was he really afraid?

And in his dejection he felt quite sure that he was afraid of nothing; that he was profoundly indifferent, full of an intolerable weariness of self-torture. He was too tired to feel alarm; he would wait and see what would happen. It must come. There was no escape. It was Fatality. It was rest to sit there, motionless, inert, will-less, with the wide silver-gray waters before him, waiting for what might happen. To struggle no more for his own ends, to fear no more, but to wait patiently and forever. It must come, like the tide from the ocean; it must cover him, as the surf covers the sands—and then go down again, and perhaps drag him with it, drowned and dead. A wave of that flood would wash over him and stop his breath—and more waves would follow—endlessly. A senseless tide—a fruitless eternity.

"I wish I did not feel it so acutely," he painfully thought. "It is too silly to feel it so. Perhaps nothing will come of it, and I shall live to be a hundred, in peace and contentment. Still, this is undeniable, this is a fact: they are there! They are here! But—if It were really coming I

Fate

should not feel it. Nothing happens but the un-
expected. It is mere nervous weakness, over-
tension. Nothing can really matter to me; nothing
matters. The air is lovely and pleasantly soft;
there floats a cloud. And I will just sit still, without fear, quite at my ease. There they are again!
The seamews fly low— I will wait, wait—
Those boys are playing in that boat; what folly!
They will have it over!"

He looked with involuntary interest at their an-
tics, and then again at the gentleman and lady.
They were now full in sight, just below him; and
they went past, knowing nothing, without a gesture, like two puppets.

"Ah! but *I* know," thought he. "They are here,
and It has come in their train perhaps. But it may
go away with them too, and be no more than a
threat. So I shall wait; I do not care. If it must
come it must."

They had gone out of sight. The boys and their
boat were gone too. The shore in front of him was
lonely—a long stretch of desert. Suddenly he was
seized with a violent shivering—an ague. He
stood up, his face quite colorless, his knees quaking. Terror had suddenly been too much for
him, and large beads of sweat bedewed his forehead.

"God above!" thought he, "life is terrible. I
have made it terrible. I am afraid. What can I

do? Run away? No, no; I must wait. Can any harm come to me? No, none! None, none— There they were both of them, she and her father. I am really afraid. Oh! if it must come, great God! only let it come quickly!"

Then he fancied his eyes had deceived him; that it had not been those two. Impossible! And yet he knew that they were there. Terror throbbed in his breast with vehement heart-beating, and he now only marveled that he could have looked at the boat with the boys at all, while Sir Archibald and Eva were walking down on the shore: would it not be upset? That was what he had been thinking of the boat.

Fate

CHAPTER XXVI

A WHOLE fortnight of broiling summer days slipped by; and he waited, always too weary to make the smallest effort to induce Frank to quit the place. It might perhaps have cost him no more than a single word. But he never spoke the word —waiting, and gradually falling under a spell of waiting, as though he were looking for the mysterious outcome of an interesting *dénouement.* Had they already met anywhere? Would they meet? And if they should, would anything come of it? One thing inevitably follows another, thought he; nothing can ever be done to check their course.

Westhove was in the habit of remaining a great deal indoors, leading a quiet life between his gloomy thoughts and his favorite gymnastics, not troubling himself about the summer crowd outside on the terrace and the shore. Thus the fortnight passed without his becoming aware of the vicinity of the woman whom Van Maeren dreaded. Not a suspicion of premonition thrilled through Frank's mild melancholy; he had gone on breathing the fresh sea air without perceiving any fragrance in the atmosphere that could suggest her presence.

Fate

He did not discern the prints of her little shoes on the level strand below the villa, nor the tilt of her parasol passing under his eyes, as he sat calmly smoking with his feet on the railings. And they must often have gazed at the selfsame packet steaming into the narrow harbor, like a colored silhouette cut out of a print, with its little sails and flag of smoke, but their eyes were unconscious how nearly they must be crossing each other, out there over the sea.

After these two scorching weeks there came a dull, gray, sunless day, with heavy rain stored in the driving black clouds, like swollen water-skins.

Frank had gone for a walk on the shore, by the edge of the wailing, fretting sea; the basket-chairs had been carried higher up, and were closely packed and almost unoccupied. There was scarcely any one out. A dismal sighing wind swept the waters; it was an autumn day full of the desolation of departed summer joys. And as he walked on, his ears filled with the moaning breeze, he saw her coming toward him with waving skirts and fluttering ribbons, and—Great Heaven! it was she!

It was as though a mass of rock had been suddenly cast at his breast with a giant's throw, and he lay crushed and breathless beneath. A surge of mingled joy and anguish struggled through his pulses, thrilled his nerves, mounted to his brain.

Fate

He involuntarily stood still, and almost unconsciously exclaimed, in a tone inaudible, indeed, at any distance, and drowned in the wind:

"Eva! My God! Eva!"

But the distance was lessening; now she was close to him, and apparently quite calm; because she had already seen him that very morning, though he had not seen her; because she had gone through the first emotion; because she had walked that way, in the wind, close by the villa into which she had seen him vanish, in the hope of meeting him again. The question flashed through his mind whether he should greet her with a bow, as a stranger—doing it with affected indifference, as though unmoved by this accidental meeting and forgetful of the past. And in spite of his tremulous excitement he could still be amazed at seeing her come straight toward him, without any hesitation, as if to her goal. In an instant she stood before him, with her pale, earnest face, and dark eyes beaming with vitality; he saw her whole form and figure, absorbed them into himself, as though his soul would devour the vision.

"Frank," she said, softly.

He made no reply, shivering with emotion, and scarcely able to see through the mist of tears which dimmed his eyes. She smiled sadly.

"Will you not hear me?" she said, in her low, silvery voice.

Fate

He bowed, awkwardly muttering something, awkwardly putting out his hand. She gently grasped it, and went on, still in that subdued tone like an echo:

"Do not be vexed with me for addressing you. There is something I should like to say to you. I am glad to have met you here in Scheveningen by mere chance—or perhaps not by mere chance. There was some misunderstanding, Frank, between you and me, and unpleasant words were spoken on both sides. We are parted, and yet I should like to ask your forgiveness for what I then said."

Tears choked her; she could scarcely control herself; but she concealed her emotion and stood calmly before him; brave as women can be brave, and with that sad smile full of hopeless submission, without affectation, candid and simple.

"Do not take it amiss; only let me ask you whether you can forgive me for having once offended you, and will henceforth think of me more tenderly."

"Eva, Eva!" he stammered. "You ask me to forgive? It was I—it was I who—"

"Nay," she gently interrupted, "you have forgotten. It was I—do you forgive me?" And she held out her hand. Frank wrung it, with a sob that choked in his throat.

"Thank you. I am glad," she went on. "I was in the wrong; why should I not confess it? I own

Fate

it frankly— Will you not come and see papa? We are living in a *hôtel garni*. Have you anything to do? If not, come now with me. Papa will be very pleased to see you."

"Certainly, of course," he muttered, walking on by her side.

"But I am not taking you from any one else? Perhaps some one is waiting for you. Perhaps now—by this time—you are married."

She forced herself to look at him with her faint smile—a languid, pale courtesy which parted her lips but sadly; and her voice was mildly blank, devoid of any special interest. He started at her words; they conveyed a suggestion which had never occurred to him; a strange idea transferred from her to him; but it took no root, and perished instantly.

"Married! Oh, Eva—no, never!" he exclaimed.

"Well, such a thing might have been," said she, coolly.

They were silent for a while; but in a few moments, Eva, touched by the tone of his last words, could no longer contain herself, and began to cry gently, like a frightened child, sobbing spasmodically as they walked on, the tears soaking her white gauze veil.

In front of their hotel she stopped, and, controlling herself for a moment, said:

"Frank, be honest with me: do you not think it

odious of me to have spoken to you? I could not make up my mind what I ought to do; but I so much wanted to confess myself wrong, and ask you to forgive me. Do you despise me for doing such a thing which, perhaps, some other girl would never have done?"

"Despise you! I despise you?" cried he, with a gulp. But he could say no more, for some visitors were coming toward them—though but few were out on this windy and threatening day. They went a little further, hanging their heads like criminals under the eyes of the strangers. Then they turned into the hotel.

Fate

CHAPTER XXVII

SIR ARCHIBALD received Frank somewhat coolly, though civilly. Then he left them together, and Eva at once began:

"Sit down, Frank. I have something to tell you."

He obeyed in some surprise; her tone was business-like, her emotion was suppressed, and she seemed to be prepared to make some clear and logical statement.

"Frank," said she, "you once wrote a letter to papa, did you not?"

"Yes," he nodded sadly.

"You did?" she exclaimed eagerly.

"Yes," he repeated. "Two to you and one to Sir Archibald."

"What! and two to me as well?" she cried in dismay.

"Yes," he nodded once more.

"And you had no answers," she went on, more calmly. "Did you ever wonder why?"

"Why?" he echoed in surprise. "Because you were offended—because I had been so rough—"

Fate

"No," said she, very positively. "Simply and solely because we never received your letters."

"What?" cried Westhove.

"They never reached us. Our servant William seems to have had some interest in keeping them back."

"Some interest?" repeated Frank, dully, bewildered. "Why?"

"That I do not know," replied Eva. "All I know is this: our maid Kate—you remember her —came crying one day to tell me that she could not stay any longer, for she was afraid of William, who had declared that he would murder her. I inquired what had happened; and then she told me that she had once been just about to bring up a letter to papa—in your handwriting. She knew your writing. William had come behind her when she was close to the door, and had snatched it from her, saying that he would carry it in; but instead of doing so he had put the letter into his pocket. She had asked him what he meant by it; then they had a violent quarrel, and ever since she had been afraid of the man. She had wanted to tell me a long time ago, but dared not for fear of William. We questioned William, who was rough and sulky, and considered himself offended by our doubts of his honesty. Papa had his room searched to see if he had stolen any more letters or other things. Nothing, however, was to be found, neither stolen articles nor letters. Not even the letter to papa, which seems to have been the last of the three you wrote."

"It was," said Frank.

"Of course papa dismissed the man. And—oh, what was it I wanted to tell you?—I can not remember— So you wrote actually three times?"

"Indeed, I did; three times."

"And what did you say?" she asked, with a sob in her throat.

"I asked you to forgive me, and whether—whether all could not be the same again. I confessed that I had been wrong—"

"But you were not."

"Perhaps not. I can not tell now. I felt it so then. I waited and waited for a word from you or your father. And none came."

"No, none!" she sighed. "And then?"

"What could I have done?"

"Why did you not come yourself? Oh! why did you never come near us?" she wailed reproachfully.

He was silent for a minute, collecting his thoughts; he could not remember it all.

"Tell me, Frank?" she said softly. "Why did you not come yourself?"

"I can not remember exactly," he said, dully.

"Then you did think of it?"

"Yes, certainly," said he.

Fate

"Then how was it that you never came?"

Frank suddenly broke down; he gulped down his tears with difficulty, a gulp of anguish.

"Because I was heart-broken, because I was so wretched, so unspeakably wretched. I had always taken rather cynical views of women, and love, and so forth; and then when I met you it was all so new, so fresh to me, I felt myself a boy again; I was in love with you, not only for your beauty, but for everything you said and did; for being what you are, always so calm and sweet. Good God! I adored you, Eva— Then there was that change: that doubt, that dreadful time. I can not remember it all now; and I felt so forlorn and broken-hearted. I could have died then, Eva, Eva!"

"You were so miserable? And you did not come to me?"

"No."

"But, good heavens, why not?"

"I wanted to go to you."

"And why did you not do it, then?" Again he sat lost in thought; his brain seemed clouded.

"Ah, yes! I think I remember all about it now," he said slowly. "I wanted to go—and then Bertie said—"

"What did Bertie say?"

"That he thought me a fool for my pains; a coward, and a cur, and a fool."

Fate

"But why?"

"Because you had disbelieved my word."

"And then?"

"I thought perhaps he was right and I did not go."

She flung herself on a sofa in utter woe, weeping passionately.

"Then it was what Bertie said?" she cried reproachfully.

"Yes; nothing else," he said, mournfully. "God in heaven! that alone."

They were both silent. Then Eva sat upright again, shivering; her face was white and bloodless, her eyes fixed with a dull, vacant glare, like weathered glass.

"Oh, Frank!" she cried—"Frank, I am so frightened! It is coming!"

"What, what?" he asked in alarm.

"I feel it coming upon me!" she moaned, panting. "It is like the sound of distant thunder, droning in my ears and in my brain. Great Heavens! It is close to me! Frank, oh, Frank! It is above me, over me. The thunder is over my head!" She shrieked and fought the air with her arms as if to beat something off, and her slender frame was convulsed as from a series of mysterious electric shocks. Her breath came rattling in her throat. Then she tottered, and he thought she would have fallen. He clasped her in his arms.

Fate

"Eva, Eva!" he cried.

She allowed him to drag her to the sofa without making any resistance, happy in his embrace in spite of her hallucination; and there she remained, sitting by him, with his arm round her, cowering against his breast.

"Eva! come, Eva, what is it that ails you?"

"It has passed over," she murmured, almost inaudibly. "Yes, it is gone now—it is gone. It has come over me so often lately; it comes roaring on, slowly and stealthily, and then it breaks over my head, shaking me to the core; and then it goes away, dies away—away— I am in such terror of it; it is like a monster which comes bellowing at me, and it frightens me so! What can it be?"

"I can not tell; overwrought nerves, perhaps," he said, consolingly.

"Oh! hold me close," she said, caressingly; "hold me tightly to you. When I am alone after it is past, I am left in such deadly fear; but now—now I have you—you once more. You will not cast me from you again; you will protect me, your poor little Eva, will you not? Ah! yes, I have you back now. I knew, I felt, I should have you back some day; and I have made papa come to Scheveningen every summer. I had an idea that you must be somewhere in Holland—at The Hague or at Scheveningen; and that if we were ever to meet again it would be here. And now it has happened,

and I have you once more. Hold me tightly now
—in both arms—both arms. Then I shall not be
frightened."

She clung more closely to his breast, her head
on his shoulder; and then, in a voice like a child's:

"Look," she said, holding out her wrist.

"What?" asked he.

"That little scar. You did that."

"I did?"

"Yes; you clutched me by the wrists."

He felt utterly miserable, in spite of having
found her again, and he covered the line of the
scar with little kisses.

She laughed quietly.

"It is a bracelet!" she said lightly.

Fate

CHAPTER XXVIII

Presently, however, he started up.

"Eva," he began, suddenly recollecting himself, "how—why—?"

"What is it?" she said, laughing, but a little exhausted after her strange fear of the fancied thunder.

"Those letters. Why did William?—what could they matter to William? Not mere curiosity to see what was in them?"

"He would not have snatched that last one so roughly from Kate, if that had been all. No, no—"

"Then you think he had some interest?"

"I do."

"But what? Why should he care whether I wrote to you or no?"

"Perhaps he was acting for—"

"Well?"

"For some one else."

"But for whom? What concern could my letters be of anybody's. What advantage could it be to any one to hinder your getting them?"

She sat up and looked at him for some time

Fate

without speaking, dreading the question she must ask.

"Can you really think of no one?" she said.

"No."

"Did no one know that you had written?"

"No one but Bertie."

"Ah! Only Bertie," said she, with emphasis.

"But Bertie—no! Surely?" he asked her, indignant at so preposterous a suspicion.

"Perhaps," she whispered, almost inaudibly. "Perhaps Bertie."

"Eva! Impossible. Why? How?"

She sank back into her former attitude, her head on his breast, trembling still from the impression of the thunder she had heard. And she went on:

"I know nothing; I only think. I have thought it over day after day for two years; and I have begun to find a great deal that seems mysterious in what had never before been puzzling, but, indeed, sympathetic to me—in Bertie. You know we often used to talk together, and sometimes alone. You were a little jealous sometimes, but you had not the smallest reason for it, for there never was anything to make you so; we were like a brother and sister. We often talked of you— Well, afterward I remembered those talks, and it struck me that Bertie—"

"Yes? That Bertie—"

"That he did not speak of you as a true friend

should. I am not sure. While he was talking it never occurred to me, for Bertie had a tone, and a way of saying things. I always fancied then that he meant well by us both, and that he really cared for us, but that he was afraid of something happening—some evil, some catastrophe, if we were married. He seemed to think that we ought not to marry. When afterward I thought over what he had said that was always the impression. He really seemed to think that we—that we ought never to be married."

She closed her eyes, worn out by this effort to solve the enigmas of the past, and she took his hand and stroked it as she held it in her own. He too tried to look into that labyrinth of the past, but he could discern nothing. His memory carried him back to their last days in London; and he did recall something: he recollected Van Maeren's stern tone when he, Westhove, had said he should call at the Rhodeses'; he remembered Bertie's urgent haste to get out of London and wander about the world. Could Bertie—? Had Bertie any interest? —But he could not discern it, in the simplicity of his unpractical, heedlessly liberal friendship, which had never taken any account of expenses, always sharing what he had with his companion because he had plenty and the other had nothing; he could not see it, since he had never thought of such a possibility in his strange indifference to everything that approached money matters—an indifference so complete as to constitute a mental deficiency, as another man is indifferent to all that concerns politics, or art, or what not—matters which he held so cheap, and understood so little and could only shake his head over it, as over an abracadabra. He looked, but saw not.

"You see, I fancied afterward that Bertie had been opposed to our marrying," Eva repeated dreamily; and then, bewildered by the mystery which life had woven about her, she went on: "Tell me, Frank, what was there in him? What was he, who was he? Why should you never tell me anything about him? For I discovered that too, later, during those two years when I thought out so many things."

He looked at her in dismay. Bitter self-reproach came upon him for never having told her that Bertie was poor, penniless, and dependent on his friend's bounty. Why was it he had never told her? Was it out of a sense of shame at being himself so careless, so foolishly weak about a concern in which others were so cautious and prudent? So foolishly weak—careless to imbecility. And still he looked at her in dismay.

Then a suspicion of the truth flashed across his mind like the zigzag glimmer of distant lightning, and he shrank from its lurid gleam.

"Eva," he said, "I will go to Bertie—"

Fate

"To Bertie?" she shrieked. "Is he here?"

"Yes."

"He! here! Oh, I had never thought of that. I fancied he was away, far away—dead perhaps. I did not care what had become of him. Great God! Here! Frank, I implore you, Frank, leave him; do not go near him."

"But, Eva, I must ask him."

"No, Frank—oh, Frank, for God's sake, do not go. I am afraid—afraid. Do not go."

He soothed her gently with a soft, sad smile which just lifted his yellow mustache; with grave fondness in his honest eyes; he soothed and petted her very gently, to reassure her.

"Do not be afraid, my darling. I will be quite calm. But still I must ask, don't you see? Wait for me here; I will return in the evening."

"Can you really be calm? Oh, you had better not go—"

"I promise you I will be quite calm, quite cool." And he embraced her fondly, closely, with passionate fervor.

"Then you are mine once more?" he asked.

She threw her arms round his neck, and kissed his lips, his eyes, his face.

"Yes," she said, "I am yours. Do what you will with me."

"Till we meet again," then said he; and he quitted the house.

Fate

Eva, left alone, looked about her with a shudder, as if seeking the evil she dreaded. She was afraid—afraid for herself and for Frank, but chiefly for Frank. In an instant her fears had risen to intolerable horror. She heard her father's step in the passage: she recognized his shuffling tread. It was impossible for her to meet him just then; she snatched up a cloak and wrapped it about her, pulling the hood over her head, as she rushed out of doors.

It was raining heavily.

Fate

CHAPTER XXIX

FRANK found Van Maeren at home. And Bertie saw at once that it had come. He read it in Frank's drawn face, heard it in the thick utterance of his voice. And at the same time he felt that the lax springs of his determination were trying to brace themselves in despair, in self-defense, and—that they failed.

"Bertie," said Westhove. "I want to speak to you, to ask you something."

Bertie made no reply. His legs quaked. He was sitting in a large cane chair, and he did not move.

"I have just met Eva," Frank went on, "and I went with her to see her father. Sir Archibald tells me that they have been here some weeks—"

Still Bertie spoke not; he gazed up at Frank with his deep, black eyes, and their brilliancy was overcast by distress and fear. Frank stood in front of him, and he now passed his hand over his brow in some confusion. He had at first purposed to tell his story, and then, quite calmly, to ask a question; but something, he knew not what, in Bertie's cat-like indolence, roused his anger, made

Fate

him furious with him for the first time in all the years he had known him. He was angry that Bertie could stay there, half lying down languidly at ease, his graceful hand hanging over the arm of the lounge; and he did not detect that his attitude at this moment was assumed merely to conceal an all too overwhelming agitation. And Frank's intention of telling a logical tale and asking a plain question suddenly collapsed in rage, giving way to a mad desire to know at once—at once—

"Listen to me, Bertie. You remember the three letters that I wrote before we left London. Eva tells me that they were kept back by their servant, William. Do you know anything about it?"

Bertie was silent, but his eyes were fixed on Frank with dull, anxious entreaty.

"No one knew of the existence of those letters but you. Have you any suspicion why it should be to William's interest to suppress them, then?"

"No. How should I?" said Bertie, scarcely above his breath.

"Come, come—speak out!" cried Westhove, quivering in every muscle. "You must know something about it, that is quite clear. You must. Speak out."

All thought of self-defense melted away under the vehemence of Frank's tone. Bertie hardly had any curiosity even to know what had occurred to

Fate

betray William's complicity; and he felt that it would be easiest now to give himself up completely, without reserve, since that which he had been dreading for weeks had come upon him, inevitably and fatally; since whatever was to happen would happen inevitably and fatally; and in his weakness he was conscious of the horrible pathos, the hopeless pity of his being what he was—of things being as they were.

"Well, then," he muttered, dejectedly, "I do know."

"What do you know?"

"It was I who—"

"Who did what?"

"Who bribed William not to deliver the letters."

Westhove looked at him in dumb astonishment; darkness clouded his sight; everything was in a whirl; he did not hear, did not understand, forgetting that the truth had already flashed across his brain.

"You! You!" he gasped. "My God! but why?"

Van Maeren got up; he burst into tears.

"Because—because—I don't know. I can not tell you. It is too vile."

Westhove had seized him by the shoulders: he shook him, and said in a hoarse roar:

"You damned villain, you will not tell me why? You will not tell me? Or must I shake it out of your body? Why? Tell me this instant!"

Fate

"Because, because," sobbed Van Maeren, wringing his white hands.

"Tell me—out with it!"

"Because I wanted to stay with you, and because if you married I should have had to go. I was so fond of you, and—and—"

"Speak out! You were so fond of me—and then—"

"And you were so kind to me. You gave me everything. I foresaw that I should have to work for my living again, and I was so well off where I was. Frank, Frank, listen to me; hear what I have to tell you before you say anything, before you are angry. Let me explain; do not condemn me till you know. Oh, yes, it was base of me to do what I did, but let me say a word; and do not be angry, Frank, till you know everything. Frank, try to see me as I am. I am as God made me, and I can not help it; I would have been different if I could—and I only did what I could not help doing. Indeed, I could not help it; I was driven to it by a power outside me. I was so weak, so tired; I could rest with you; and though you may not believe me, I loved you, I worshiped you. And you wanted to turn me out, and make me work. Then it was—then I did it. Hear me, Frank, let me tell you all. I must tell you all. I made Eva believe that you did not really love her; I made her doubt you, so that everything was broken off between you. And the letters, I stopped them— It was all my doing, Frank, all, all; and I hated myself while I did it, because I was not different from what I am. But, I could not help it. I was made so— And you do not understand me. I am such a strange mixture that you can not understand. But try to understand me and you will, Frank; and then you will forgive me—perhaps you will even forgive me. Oh, believe me, I beseech you, I am not wholly selfish. I love you with all my soul, so truly as one man hardly ever loves another, because you were so good to me. I can prove it to you; did I not stick by you when you had lost all your money in America? If I had been selfish, should I not have left you then? But I stayed with you, I worked with you, and we shared everything, and were happy. Oh, why did not things remain as they were? Now you have met her, and now—"

"Have you done with words!" roared Frank. "So you did this, you wrecked all that life held for me! God in heaven! is it possible? No, you are right; I do not understand you!" he ended with a venomous laugh, his face crimson and his eyes starting with rage. Bertie had dropped crouching in a heap on the ground, and sobbed aloud.

"Oh, but try to understand," he entreated. "Try to see a fellow-creature as he is, in all his comfortless nakedness, with no conventional wrap-

pings. My God! I swear to you that I wish I
was different. But how can I help being what I
am? I was born without any option of my own;
I was endowed with a brain and I must think; and
I think otherwise than I gladly would think,
and I have been tossed through life like a ball—
like a ball. What could I do, thus tossed, but try
to keep my head up? Strength of will, strength of
mind? I do not know whether you have any; but
I have never, never, never felt such a thing. When
I do a thing it is because I must, because I can do
no otherwise; for though I may have the wish to
act differently the strength and energy are not
there! Believe me, I despise myself; believe
that, Frank; and try to understand and to forgive."

"Words, words! You are raving," growled
Frank. "I do not know what all your talk means.
I can understand nothing at this moment; and,
even if I could, at this moment I would not. All
I understand is that you have ruined me, that you
have destroyed my whole life's joy, and that you
are a low scoundrel, who bribed a servant to stop
my letters, out of gross, vile, unfathomable selfishness. Bribed him? Tell me, rascal, wretch, coward—bribed him!—with what, in Heaven's name?
Tell me with what you bribed him."

"With, with—" but Van Maeren hesitated in
abject fear, for Westhove had collared him by the

Fate

waistcoat, as he groveled on the floor, and shook him again and again.

"By thunder, you villain, you bribed him with my money—with my own money! Tell me—speak, or I'll kick it out of you!"

"Yes."

"With my money?"

"Yes, yes, yes." Frank flung him down with a yell of contempt, of loathing of such a thing as he.

But Van Maeren was experiencing a reaction from his self-abasement. The world was so stupid, men were stupid, Frank was stupid. He did not understand that a man should be such as he, Bertie, was; he could not understand; he bellowed out in his brutal rage, like some wild beast without brains or sense. He, himself, had brains; happier was he who had none; he envied Frank his lack of them!

He sprang up with one leap.

"Yes, if you will have it! Yes, yes, yes!" he hissed it hard. "If you don't understand, if you are too idiotic to take it in— Yes, I say! Yes, yes, yes! I bribed him with your money, that you were so kind as to give me the very last day when we were leaving London. You gave me a hundred pounds, to pay William—do you remember? To pay William!— You do not understand? Well—you don't understand! You are a stupid brute without brains. Ay, and I envy you for having none. There was a time when I had none; and

Fate

do you know how I came by them? Why, through you. There was a time when I toiled and worked, and never thought and never cared. I ate all I earned, and when I earned nothing I went hungry. And I was happy! It was you—you who fed me on dainties, and gave me wine to drink; and it was you who clothed me, so that I had not to work, but had nothing to do but to think, think, in my contemptible idleness all day long. And now I only wish I could crack my skull open and throw my brains in your face for having made me what I am, so finikin and full of ideas! You don't understand? Then perhaps you will not understand that at this moment I feel no gratitude for all you have done for me—that I hate you for it all, that I despise you, and that you have made my life infinitely more wretched than I have made yours! Do you understand that much, at any rate, eh? That I despise you and hate you, hate you?"

He had entrenched himself behind a table, sputtering out this volley of words in a paroxysm of nervous excitement; he felt as though every fibre of his frame was ready to crack like an overstrained cord. He had got behind the table, because Westhove was standing before him, at the other side now, his eyes staringly white and bloodshot in his purple face; his nostrils dilated, his shoulders up, his fists clenched, ready, as it seemed, to spring upon him. Westhove was waiting, as it appeared, till Van Maeren had spit out in his face all the foul words he could find.

"Yes, I hate you!" Bertie repeated, "I hate you!" He could find nothing else to say.

Then Frank let himself go. With a bellow like a wild beast, a sound that had nothing human in it, he sprang over the table, which tilted on its side, and came down with all the weight of his impetus on Bertie, who fell under him like a reed. He seized his foe by the throat, dragged him over the legs of the table, into the middle of the room, dropped him with a crack on the floor, and fell upon him, with his bony, square knee on Bertie's chest, and his left hand holding his neck like a vise. And a hard, dry feeling, like a thirst for sheer brutality, rose to Westhove's throat; with a dreadful smile on his lips he swallowed two or three times, fiendishly glad that he had him in his power, in the clutch of his left hand, under his knee. And he doubled his right fist and raised it like a hammer, with a tigerish roar.

"There, there, there!" he growled; and each time a sledge-hammer blow fell on Bertie. "There, there, there!"—on his nose, his eyes, his mouth, his forehead—and the blows resounded dully on his skull, as if on metal. A red mist clouded Westhove's sight; everything was red—purple, scarlet, vermilion. A blood-stained medley circled round him like whirling wheels, and through that strange

Fate

crimson halo a distorted face grinned up at him under the pounding of his fist. The corners of the room swam in red, as if they were full of tangible red terror, whirling, whirling round him—a purple dizziness, a scarlet madness, a nightmare bathed in blood; and his blows fell fast and steadily—"there!—there!—there!"—and his left hand closed tighter on the delicate white throat below that face—

The door flew open, and she, Eva, rushed up to him through the red mist, parting it, dispelling it by the swift actuality of her appearance.

"Frank, Frank!" she screamed. "Stop, I entreat you! Stop! You are murdering him!"

He let his arm drop, and looked at her as in a dream. She tried to drag him back, to get him away from the battered body, to which he clung in his fury like a vampire.

"Leave him, Frank, I beseech you; let him stand up. Do not kill him. I was outside, and I was frightened. I did not understand, because you were speaking Dutch. Great Heavens! What have you done to him? Look, look! What a state he is in!"

Frank had risen to his feet, dazed by that red frenzy; he had to lean on the table.

"I have given him what he deserved—I have thrashed him, and I will do it again!"

He was on the point of falling on the foe once

more, with that devilish grin on his face and that brutal thirst still choking him.

"Frank, no! Frank!" cried Eva, clinging to him with both hands. "For God's sake be satisfied! Look at him! oh, look at him!' '

"Well, then, let him get up," Frank snarled. "He may get up. Get up, wretch, at once; get up!"

He gave him a kick—and a second—and a third —to make him rise. But Van Maeren did not move.

"Great God! only look at him," said Eva, kneeling down by the body. "Look—don't you see?" She turned to Frank, and he, as if awaking from his dream of blood, did see now, and saw with horror. There it lay: the legs and arms convulsed and writhing, the body breathlessly still in the loose, light-hued summer suit; and the face a mask of blue and green and violet, stained with purplish blood, which oozed from ears and nose and mouth, trickling down, clammy and dark, drop by drop, on to the carpet. One eye was a shapeless mass, half pulp and jelly; the other stared out of the oval socket like a large, dull, melancholy opal. The throat looked as though it had a very broad purple band round it. And as they stood gazing down at the features it seemed that they were swelling, swelling to a sickening, unrecognizable deformity.

Fate

Out of doors the storm of rain had not ceased. There they stood, staring at the horror that lay bleeding and motionless on the ground before them; a leaden silence within, and without the falling torrent, an endless, endless plash.

Eva, kneeling by Bertie's side, and shuddering with terror, had felt his heart, had listened with her ear against the breathless trunk—close to the dreadful thing, to make sure—and she had got up again quaking, had very softly stepped back from it, her eyes still directed on it, and now stood clinging against Frank, as if she would become one with him in her agony of fear.

"Frank," she gasped. "God have mercy! Frank! He is dead! Let us go—let us go; let us fly!"

"Is he dead?" asked Westhove, dully. His mind was beginning to wake—a faint dawn like murky daybreak. He released himself from her grasp; knelt down, listened, felt, thought vaguely of fetching a doctor, of remedies; and then he added huskily, certain, indeed, of what he said, but quite uncertain of what he should do:

"Yes, he is dead—he is dead. What can I—?"

Eva still hung on to him, imploring him to fly, to escape. But his mind was gradually getting clearer, daylight shining in on his bewilderment; he freed himself from her embrace, and tried to go; his hand was already on the door-handle.

193

Fate

"Frank, Frank!" she shrieked, for she saw that he meant to abandon her.

"Hush!" he whispered, with a finger on his lips. "Stay here; stay and watch him. I will come back."

And he went. She would have followed him, have clung to him in an agony of terror, but he had already shut the door behind him, and her trembling knees could scarcely carry her. She sat down by the body, shivering miserably. There it was—the swollen, bruised, and purple face, sad, and sickening in the diffused afternoon light which came in obliquely through the curtain of rain. Every breath stuck in her throat; she was dying for air, and longed to open the window, being closer to that than to the door.

But she dared not; for outside, through the dim square panes, she saw the tragical sky covered with driving slate-colored piles of cloud, and the rain falling in a perfect deluge, and the sea dark and ominous as an imminent threat, the raging foam gleaming through a shroud of pouring water.

"Molde, Molde!" she exclaimed, icy-cold with terrible remembrance. "It is the sky of Molde, the fjord of Molde! That was where I first felt it. O God! Help, help!"

And she fell senseless on the floor.

Fate

CHAPTER XXX

SINCE that day of terror two years had elapsed, years of silent endurance for them both; each suffering alone. For they were parted; with only the solace of a brief meeting now and then, when she could go and see him where he was spending those two years, the days slowly dragging past, in the prison among the sand-hills.

He had given himself up at once to the police of Scheveningen, as if he were walking in his sleep, and had been taken to the House of Detention. He had stood his trial—it had lasted six weeks, a short time, his lawyer had said to comfort him, because there was no mystery to clear up; the murder was proved to a demonstration, beyond the shadow of a doubt, to be the result of a quarrel. This was evident also from the evidence of Miss Rhodes, who had stated that the criminal himself had not at first understood that his friend was dead, for that he had immediately after kicked him two or three times to rouse him, thinking he was only in a state of collapse; and that this had taken place in her presence. The trial was watched with

Fate

interest by the public; and their sympathy was aroused when the purchase of the letters came out through the evidence of Sir Archibald and his daughter, confirmed by William, whose presence was secured by diplomatic interference. There were no difficulties; six weeks settled everything. Frank was sentenced to two years' imprisonment, and the case was not taken to a higher court.

He had spent the time, day after day, in a waking dream of gloomy lucidity, with always, always the sinister vision of that writhing body, and the horror of that dreadful battered face before his eyes. He had felt it glide over the pages of his book when he tried to read, among the letters he traced when he tried to write—what he scarcely knew, fragments of an account of his travels through America and Australia—a melancholy employment and full of pain, since every word reminded him of the murdered man who had been his constant companion. And when he did nothing, but gazed in dreary reverie out of the window of his cell, there, just below, and not very far away, he could see the villa where they had dwelt together and where he had done the deed, with a glimmer of the sea, a shining gray streak; and in fancy he could smell the briny scent, as in the days when he had spent hour after hour, with his feet on the balustrade—the hours which, as they crept on, though he knew it not, were bringing inevitable

Fate

doom on them both, every moment nearer. So it never left him; it haunted him incessantly.

Eva had entreated her father to remain at The Hague during all this terrible time, and Sir Archibald had consented, fearing for his daughter's health. Her natural sweet equanimity had given way to a fitful nervousness, which tormented her with hallucinations, visions of thunder and of blood. So they had settled in the Van Stolk Park, and all through Frank's imprisonment she had been able to see him from time to time, coming home more exhausted from each visit, in despair over his melancholy, however she might try to encourage him with hopes for the future, later on, when he should be free. She herself could hope, nay, lived only on hope; controlling her excitability under the yoke of patience, and of her confidence in something brighter which might come into her life, by and by, when Frank was free. A new life! Oh, for a new life! and her spirits danced at the thought—and new happiness! Great God! some happiness! She did not herself understand how she could still hope, since she had known so much of life and of men, and since she had lived through that fearful experience; but she would not think of it, and in the distant future she saw everything fair and good. Even her hallucinations did not destroy her hopefulness; though dreading them, she regarded them as a recurring

malady of the brain, which would presently depart
of itself. She could even smile as she sat dreaming in the pale light of a starlit summer evening,
the calendar in her hand, on which she scratched
through each day as it died, with a gold pencil-case
which she had bought on purpose and used for
nothing else, wearing it in a bracelet;—struck it
out, with a glad, firm stroke, as bringing her nearer
to the blissful future. And she would even let the
days pass without erasing them severally, that she
might have the joy at the end of a week of making
six or seven strokes, one after another, in a luxury
of anticipation.

And now, long as they had been, the days had
all stolen by—all, one after another, beyond recall.
The past was more and more the past, and would
forever remain so; it would never come back to
them, she thought, never haunt them more with
hideous memories. She grew calmer; her nervousness diminished, and something like peace
came upon her in her passionate longing for the
happy future; for she was going to be happy with
Frank.

She was now in London again with her father,
living very quietly; still feeling the past, in spite
of her present gladness, still conscious of what had
been, in all its misery and its horror. Frank, too,
was in London, in a poorly paid place as assistant
overseer in some engineering works, the only open-

Fate

ing he could find by the help of his old connections; jumping at it, indeed, in consideration of his antecedents, of which he had no cause to be proud. By and by he should get something better, something more suited to his attainments. And he took up his studies again to refresh his technical knowledge, which had grown somewhat rusty.

Sir Archibald had grown much older, and was crippled by attacks of rheumatism; but he still sat poring over his heraldic studies. Living in Holland for his daughter's sake, he had too long been out of his own circle of acquaintance and groove of habit; and though he had from time to time, in a fit of childish temper, expressed his vexation at Eva's becoming the wife of a murderer, he now agreed to everything, shrinking from the world and troubling himself about nothing; only craving to be left undisturbed in the apathy of his old age. "He knew nothing about it; old men know nothing of such things. The young people might please themselves; they always knew best and must have their own way." So he grumbled on, apparently indifferent, but glad at heart that Eva should marry Frank, since Frank, if he could be violent, was good at heart; and Eva would be well cared for, and he himself would have some one to bear him company in his own house—yes, yes, a little company.

Frank and Eva met but rarely during the week,

for he was busy even in the evenings, but they
saw each other regularly on Sundays. And Eva
had the whole week in which to think over the
Sunday when she had last seen him, and she tried
to recall every word that he had said, every look
he had given her. On these treasures she lived all
the week. She had never loved him so dearly as
now, when crushing depression weighed on him,
which she longed to lighten by the solace of her
love. There was something motherly in her feeling for him, as though his sufferings had made
a child of him, needing a tenderer regard than of
yore. She had loved him then for the mysterious
charm, as it seemed to her, of the contrast between
his feeble gentleness and his powerful physique;
and now it was no more than a higher development of the same charm, since she saw the stalwart,
strong man suffering so pitiably under the memory
of what he had gone through, and lacking the
energy to rise superior to it and begin life anew.
But this want of vigor did not discourage her in
her hopes for the future; on the contrary, she loved
him for his weakness, while regarding this as singular and incomprehensible in herself; dreaming
over it in her solitude, or smiling with gladness.

For she, as a woman, in spite of her nervous,
visionary temperament, could resolutely forget the
past, bravely go forward to meet the future, compelling happiness to come to her by her sweet

Fate

patience and elastic constancy. Had not all the woes of the past lain outside them both? Had not Frank done penance enough for his fit of rage to hold up his head again now? Oh, they would soon have got over it completely; they would insist on being happy, and she would cure him of everything like heart-sickness.

Thus she hoped on, a long, long time, refusing at first to acknowledge that he grew more melancholy and gloomy, sinking into deeper and deeper dejection under his burden. But at last she was compelled to see it, could no longer blind herself. She could not help seeing that he sat speechless when she talked so hopefully, listened in silence to her cheerful words and bright illusions, saying nothing, and sometimes closing his eyes with a sigh which he tried to suppress. She could not deceive herself; her sanguine moods aroused in him only an echo of despair.

And when one day this was suddenly clear to her, she felt, suddenly too, that her nervous fears had worn her out; that she was sad and ill; that her courage, her hopes, her illusions were sinking down, down, deeper and deeper. A bitterness as of wormwood rose up in her, tainting everything; she flung herself on her bed, in her loneliness, heart-broken, in utter anguish, and cursed her life, cursed God, in helpless woe.

Fate

CHAPTER XXXI

THEN, circumstances occurred which, in spite of all this, led to its being settled that they were to be married in quite a short time—in about six weeks. Frank had been helped by some of his old friends to obtain an appointment as engineer in a great Glasgow firm; Eva was to have her mother's fortune; there were no difficulties in the way.

Frank now always spent the whole of Sunday at Sir Archibald's house. He came to lunch, sitting as silent as ever, and after lunch they were usually left to themselves. At first the hours flew by, sped by Eva's day-dreams, though she was still, and in spite of herself, somewhat nervous; they would discuss various matters and even read together. But then for some little time minute would link itself to minute, while they did nothing but sit side by side on a deep sofa, holding each other's hands, and gazing into vacancy. And a moment came when they could no longer endure that grasp—no longer dared. The image of Bertie, with his purple, blood-stained face, would rise up between them; their hands parted—they were both thinking of the dead. Eva felt as if she had been an accomplice in the deed. As it grew darker intolerable misery would so overpower her that it seemed as though she must suffocate; then they would throw the windows open and stand for a long, long time to refresh themselves in the cool air, looking out over the park in the gathering gloom. She listened in dread to Frank's breath as it came and went.

Ay, and she was afraid of him, in spite of her love. After all, he had committed murder; he could do such things in his rage! Oh! if in a fit of passion she too— But she would defend herself; with the strength of despair she would cling to life. Had she not herself felt strong enough to kill?— No, no. Not she, surely. She was too timid. And, besides, she loved him so dearly; she adored him, and soon she would be his wife! Still, she was afraid.

The Sundays were no longer days so sweet as to leave a treasure of memory in which she could live through the week. On the contrary, Eva now dreaded Sunday; she awaited it with terror. . . . Friday—Saturday. . . . Here it was again! There was Frank, she heard his step. And still she was afraid, and still she loved him.

They were sitting thus one evening, hand in hand, and silent. It was still early in the afternoon, but a storm threatened, and the gray gloom peered in through the thick lace curtains. Eva, depressed by the heavy weather, thirsting for some comfort, suddenly, in spite of her fears, threw herself on Frank's breast.

"I can no longer endure this weather!" she wailed, almost moaning. "This dark, cloudy sky always oppresses me of late. I want to go to Italy, Frank, to the sun, the sun!"

He pressed her to him but did not speak. She began to weep softly.

"Say something, Frank," she sobbed.

"Yes; I do not like this heavy sky," he said, dully.

Again there was silence; she tried to control herself, clinging closely to him. Then she went on:

"I can not bear up against it; I believe since that rainy day which overtook us in Molde, so long ago now—five years and more—you remember—when we had met three or four times, a few days before, at Trondhjem?" She smiled and kissed his hand, remembering her youth: she was old now. "You recollect, we got home to the hotel drenched. I believe I have been ill ever since that day, that I took a bad cold which settled in me, though at first I did not feel it and said nothing about it, but which has been undermining me ever since, all this long time—"

He made no reply; he, too, had a vague recollection of something tragically painful at Molde, but he could no longer remember what. But she suddenly burst into a violent fit of weeping.

"Oh, Frank, speak! Say something," she besought him, in despair at his silence, feeling her terror grow greater in the stillness, and her heart throbbing wildly in spite of herself.

He passed his hand over his forehead, trying to collect his thoughts. Then he slowly replied:

"Yes, Eva—for I have something to say to you. Just this very day."

"What is that?" she asked, looking up through her tears, in surprise at his strange tone.

"I want to speak to you very seriously, Eva. Will you listen?"

"Yes."

"I want to ask you something—to ask you if you would not rather be free. To ask if you would not be glad that I should release you?"

She did not immediately understand him, and sat gazing at him open-mouthed.

"Why?" she said at length, shuddering, terrified lest he should understand something of what was torturing her soul.

"Because it would be so much better for you, my child," he said, gently. "I have no right to fetter your life to mine. I am wrecked—an old man—and you are young."

She clung closely to him.

Fate

"No, I am old, too," said she, with a smile, "and I will not have it. I will be true to you. I will always comfort you when you are out of heart. And so, together, we will both grow young again, and both be happy."

Her voice was as sweet as balm; to give him strength she felt something of her old illusions reviving in her. She would cling to him whatever the cost: she loved him.

He clasped her tightly to his breast, and kissed her fondly. For the moment she felt no fear; he was so unhappy.

"You are a dear, good girl," he whispered in a husky, trembling voice. "I do not deserve that you should be so good to me. But, seriously, Eva, think it over once more. Consider again whether you would not be unhappy, nay, wretched, if you had to be with me always. There is yet time; we have our future lives in our hands, and I can not spend mine with you, Eva, only to make yours more miserable than I have done already. So, for your sake, for your happiness, I would gladly give you back your word."

"But I will not have it!" she moaned, desperately. "I will not. I do not understand you. Why should you give me back my word?"

He took her hands caressingly in his own, and looked in her face a long time, with a sad smile under the gold-colored mustache.

Fate

"Why? Because you—because you are afraid of me, my darling."

A spasm shot through her whole frame, like an electric shock; wildly she looked at him, and wildly protested:

"It is not true, Frank; I swear it is not true! Great God! Why do you think that? What have I done to make you think it? Believe me, Frank; take my word. I swear to you by all that is holy; there. I swear to you it is not true. I am not afraid of you."

"Yes, yes, Eva, you are afraid of me," he said, calmly. "And I understand it; it must be so. And yet I assure you, you should have no cause to be. For I should be a lamb in your hands; I would lay my head in your hands; your pretty, cold, white hands, and sleep like a child. You should do with me whatever you would, and I would never be angry with you, for I could never be so again, never again. I would lie at your feet; I would feel your feet on me, on my breast, and lie so still —so calm and blessed!"

He had fallen on his knees before her, with his head in her lap, on her hands.

"Well, then," she said, gently, "if that is the case, why should I ever be afraid of you since you promise me this? And why do you talk of releasing me from my word?"

"Because I can not bear to live on, seeing you

so unhappy; because you are unhappy with me, as I can see; and because you will be even more so when we are together, later—always."

She quivered in every fibre. A strange lucidity came over her. She saw all that had happened as if mirrored in crystal.

"Hear me, Frank," she said, in a clear, bright voice. "Remain where you are and listen to me; listen well. I mean to be true to you, and we shall be happy. I feel that we shall. What has occurred that we should always be miserable? Nothing. I repeat it—nothing. Do not let us spoil our own lives. I doubted you once; you have forgiven me. That is all at an end. You discovered that Bertie was a scoundrel, and you killed him. That, too, is ended. Nothing of all this can matter to me now. I will never think of it again. It has ceased to exist so far as I am concerned. And that is all, Frank. Consider, reflect—that is all. Nothing else has happened. And that is not much. We are young and strong; we are not really old. And I tell you we can live a new life, somewhere, together; somewhere, a long way from London. A new life, Frank, a new life! I love you, Frank. You are everything to me. You are my idol, my husband, my darling, my child, my great child."

She clasped his head passionately to her bosom in a rapture, her eyes sparkling, and a flush tinging the azalea whiteness of her cheeks. But his eyes met hers with a look of anguish.

"You are an angel, Eva; you are an angel. But I can not claim you. For, listen now to me. The real truth—"

"Well, what is the truth?"

"Bertie was not a scoundrel. He was nothing but a man, a very weak man. That is the truth. Listen to me, Eva; let me speak. I thought a great deal—at Scheveningen—among the sand-hills—you know. I thought over everything I could remember of what he had said to me in those last moments, in self-defense; and by degrees all his words came back to me, and I felt that he had been in the right."

"In the right? Oh, Frank! I do not know what he said in self-defense; but now, still, shall Bertie's influence come between us to part us?" she cried, in bitter despair.

"No, it is not that," he replied. "Make no mistake; it is not Bertie's influence which divides us; it is my guilt."

"Your guilt?"

"My guilt, which rises up before me from time to time, reminding me of what I have done, so that I can not forget it, shall never forget it. Let me tell you. He was right in what he said at last. He was a weak creature, he said, flung into life without any strength of will. Was that his

fault? He despised himself for having done so
mean a thing about those letters. But he had not
known what else to do. Well, and I forgive him
for being weak, for he could not help it; and we
are all weak—I am weak, too."

"But you would never have done such a thing?"
cried Eva.

"Because I, perhaps, am different. But I am
weak all the same. I am weak when I am angry.
And then—then in my fury, I was utterly, utterly
weak. This is the truth. This is what is crushing
me; and, broken as I am, I can not be your husband. Oh, what would I not give to have him still
alive! I was fond of him once, and now I could
say to him that I do understand—that I forgive
him."

"Frank, do not be so foolish—so foolishly good,"
she exclaimed.

"Oh, it is not foolish goodness," he said, with a
melancholy smile. "It is philosophy."

"Well, then," she cried, in a hard, rough tone,
"I am no philosopher; I am not foolishly good;
I do not forgive him for being a villain, and for
making us miserable. I hate him, hate him, dead
as he is. I hate him for coming between us, and
haunting us now that you have killed him, and
for the diabolical influence he still brings to bear
on you and on me. But, I say, I will not have it,"
she shrieked despairingly, starting to her feet, but

still clinging to him. "I tell you that I will not lose you for the second time. I swear that if you try to leave me here, I will stand, holding you fast in my arms, clasping you to me till we both are dead. For I will not let him part us; I hate him! I am glad you murdered him, and if he were living now, I would do it myself. I would kill him, strangle him, strangle him!" She clenched her hands as if she gripped his throat, and held Frank in her embrace as though he were her prey.

Out of doors it was growing darker every minute.

He gently released himself, supporting her, indeed, for he felt that she was tottering in her over-tension of energy and courage. She was staring out at the weather with her sunken gray eyes, and she shivered from head to foot. He led her back to the sofa, made her sit down, and again knelt before her in more passionate devotion than ever.

"Eva!" he whispered.

"Oh, look at the clouds!" she cried. "It is pouring a deluge."

"Yes," said he. "What does that matter?—I love you."

"I can not bear up against such weather," she moaned. "It oppresses me and frightens me— oh, it terrifies me so! Protect me, Frank, shelter me; come close!"

Fate

She drew him to her on the sofa, and, opening his coat, nestled against him.

"I am so frightened. Hold me tightly—wrap your coat round me. Oh, do not let it come upon me! Lord have mercy, and do not let it come over me again, I beseech Thee!"

It was the visionary thunder she prayed to be spared. And she threw both arms round her lover, clinging to him as if to hide herself. So she remained, while he held her close; when, presently, twisting her fingers into his waistcoat-pocket, she murmured:

"What is this? what have you here?"

"What have you found?" he said, in alarm.

"This, in your waistcoat-pocket?"

"Nothing—a little vial," he muttered. "Some drops for my eyes. I have been troubled by my eyes lately."

She took out the vial. It was a tiny, dark blue bottle, with a cut-glass stopper and no label.

"For your eyes?" she said. "I did not know—"

"Yes, really," he answered. "Give it me."

But she held it hidden in her two hands, and laughed.

"No, no; I will not give it you. Why are you so uneasy? I shall not break it. Does it smell? I want to open it, but the stopper has stuck."

"Eva, I entreat you give it me," he implored her, and the perspiration stood on his brow. "It is nothing but drops for the eyes, and it has no scent. You will spill it, and it stains."

But she put her hands behind her back.

"It is not for the eyes, and you have nothing the matter with yours," she said positively.

"Yes—really—"

"No; you are deceiving me. It is—it is something else—is it not?"

"Eva, give it to me."

"Does it take effect quickly?" she asked.

"Eva, I insist. Give it me!" he repeated, angry now, and at his wits' end.

He threw his arm round her, and tried to seize her wrists; but he only grasped one empty hand, while the other flung the vial over his head on the floor. There was a little clatter of falling glass, and before he could rise she had thrown her arms round him again, dragging him down among the cushions.

"Let it lie there," she murmured with a smile. It is broken. I have broken it for you. Tell me, why did you carry that about with you?"

"It is not what you fancy," he replied, still on the defensive.

"So much the better— Why did you have it?"

He sat silent for a moment. Then, yielding to her insistence, he said:

"To take it—when all was at an end between us—in the evening, of course."

Fate

"And now you can not do so."

"Perhaps I can manage to buy some more," he said, with a gloomy laugh.

"But why is everything to be at an end between us?"

He was suddenly quite serious, mocking no more at life and death.

"For your sake, my angel; for your happiness. I beseech you, let it all be ended. Let me feel that I no longer need make you wretched. You may yet be happy; but I—I feel that everything in me hinders my ever being happy, and all happiness must begin in ourselves alone."

"And do you think I shall let you go, now that you have just told me what you would do in the evening?"

"But you are not to think that I should do it only for your sake. I always go about with that in my pocket. I have often thought of doing it; but then I have thought of you, and I lacked courage; for I know that you love me only too well."

"Not too well. I have lived in you. But for you I should never have truly lived."

"But for me you might have lived with another, and have been happy."

"No. Never with any other. That could never have been. I had to live with you. It was Fatality."

"Ay, Fatality. Bertie used to say—"

Fate

"Do not mention Bertie."

As she spoke the rain dashed against the window panes in a perfect torrent.

"It is always raining," she murmured.

"Yes—always," he mechanically repeated. She shuddered and looked in his face.

"Why do you say that?" she asked quickly.

"I do not know," said he, startled and bewildered. "I really do not know. Why, what did I say?"

They both were silent. Then she began again.

"Frank!"

"My darling."

"I will not let you leave me again. Not even for a day. I shall always be in terror for you."

"Let there be an end to everything, my child."

"No, no. Listen. Let us be together forever. Forever and ever. Let us lie down to sleep—while it is still raining."

"Eva!"

"Together. You say yourself that everything in you fails of happiness, and that nevertheless happiness must come from within. Well, it is the same with me. And yet we love each other; do we not?"

"Yes, yes."

"Then why should we remain awake in this weariful life? It is always, always raining. Give me a kiss, Frank. A good-night kiss, and let us sleep while it rains. Let me go to sleep in your arms—"

"Eva, what do you mean?" he asked, hoarsely, for he did not understand her.

"I broke the vial—broke it for you," she went on wildly. "But you can always get another!" An icy chill shot through his very marrow like a sudden frost.

"God in heaven, Eva! What do you want?" She smiled at him calmly, with a soft light in her beaming eyes, and she threw her arms round him.

"To die with you, my dearest," she whispered as in an ecstasy of joy. "What good can life do us? You were right. You can never be happy again, and I can never be happy with you. And yet I will not leave you, for you are all in all to me. Then how can we live, or why? But, oh, Frank, to die together, in each other's arms! That is the greatest bliss! A kindly poison, Frank, nothing painful. Something easy to take, that we can take together, and clasp each other, and die—die—die—" Frank shuddered with horror.

"No, Eva, no!" he cried. "You must not wish that, you can not wish that! I forbid it."

"Oh, do not forbid it," she said persuasively, falling on the floor and embracing his knees. "Let us share the same fate: that will be bliss. All about us will be rose color and gold and silver, like a glorious sunset. Oh, can you imagine anything more beautiful? Frank, that is happiness, the happiness we have looked for—which every one in this world is looking for. It is Paradise! It is Heaven!"

He was not carried away by her rapture, but her words tempted him as with the promise of a brief joy in this life and an unutterably peaceful rest in death. He could say no more to dissuade her, to check her in the heavenward flight of her fancy; but still he reflected that there were no means at hand, since the vial was broken.

Eva had risen, irresistibly attracted to the spot where the vial had fallen. She stooped and picked it up. It had fallen into the drapery of a curtain; it was not broken, only cracked and chipped. Not a drop had been spilled.

"Frank!" she screamed, in her frenzied gladness. "It is not broken! Look! It is whole. It is Fate that would not allow it to be broken."

He too was standing up, quaking with an icy chill. She had already forced out the stopper and half emptied the vial with a mad, ecstatic smile.

"Eva!" he shrieked.

And quite calmly, smiling still, she handed it to him. He looked at her for a moment, feeling as if they two were already no longer of this world, as if they were floating in a sphere of unknown natural laws, in which strange things must come to pass. The world, as it seemed, was about to perish in that deluge of pouring rain. But he saw that she stood waiting with her strange smile—and he drank—

It was quite dark; they lay on the sofa side by side, in each other's arms. He was dead. She raised her head in an agony of alarm at the storm which was raging outside, and that other storm which was raging in her dying body. The lightning glared white and the thunder was close overhead. But louder than the echoes in the air the thunder came rolling on toward Eva, nearer and nearer, louder and louder, a supernatural thunder, on the wheels of the spheres.

"It is coming!" she murmured, in the anguish of death. "Great heavens! the thunder again!"

And she sank convulsed on the body of her lover, hiding her head under his coat, to die there.

Then came a shuffling step in the passage outside the dark room. An old man's thin voice twice called the name of Eva; and a hand opened the door.